"Why in the hell did you throw me over?"

Luke muttered the question. "Why did you have to do such a terrible, destructive thing? We were made for each other."

"Oh, Luke," Katherine sighed wearily, "don't! Please don't. I can't stand raking over the past." She turned her head away, determined to resist him.

He put a hand on her loose, flowing hair and pulled her roughly to him. His hard mouth was on hers, demanding, forceful. She felt her knees go weak. She summoned up all her strength and twisted her mouth away from his.

"No, no, no," she cried. "Don't! Please. Will you please just leave me alone?" She turned angry eyes to him. "Haven't I paid enough? Aren't you satisfied?"

"Satisfied?" he drawled. "No, Katie, not until I have all of you. And I will...."

WELCOME
TO THE WONDERFUL WORLD
OF *Harlequin Romances*

Interesting, informative and entertaining,
each Harlequin Romance portrays an appealing
and original love story. With a varied array
of settings, we may lure you on an African safari,
to a quaint Welsh village, or an exotic Riviera
location—anywhere and everywhere that adventurous
men and women fall in love.

As publishers of Harlequin Romances, we're
extremely proud of our books. Since 1949,
Harlequin Enterprises has built its publishing
reputation on the solid base of quality and
originality. Our stories are the most popular
paperback romances sold in North America; every
month, six new titles are released and sold at
nearly every book-selling store in Canada and the
United States.

A free catalog listing all Harlequin Romances
can be yours by writing to the

HARLEQUIN READER SERVICE,
(In the U.S.) 2504 West Southern Avenue, Tempe, AZ 85282
(In Canada) Stratford, Ontario, N5A 6W2

We sincerely hope you enjoy reading
this Harlequin Romance.

Yours truly,

THE PUBLISHERS
Harlequin Romances

Full Circle

Rosemary Hammond

Harlequin Books

TORONTO • NEW YORK • LONDON
AMSTERDAM • PARIS • SYDNEY • HAMBURG
STOCKHOLM • ATHENS • TOKYO • MILAN

Original hardcover edition published in 1983
by Mills & Boon Limited

ISBN 0-373-02601-3

Harlequin Romance first edition February 1984

CHAPTER ONE

As she walked the short half block from the bus stop to the entrance of the Cascade Building, Katherine was already sorry she had resisted the impulse to wear her new summer suit. It was one of those unseasonably warm and sunny June days in Seattle. After weeks—months, it seemed—of constant drizzle and grey skies, the sun had suddenly burst forth yesterday afternoon and, miracle of miracles, had risen visibly again on Monday morning.

She had stood before the mirror in her bedroom this morning debating what to wear to work, always a momentous decision in Seattle's unpredictable weather. The lovely light blue shade of her new linen suit would be perfect, she had thought, maybe with the paler blue silk shirt.

For one daring moment she had even considered letting her honey coloured hair hang loose instead of pinned up in her usual severe chignon. Somehow, sunshine in Seattle, especially in June, always seemed to Katherine to call for a celebration.

As she stood there in her slip, a heavy feeling descended on her, clouding her forehead and dimming the spark in her hazel eyes. She felt a sudden need to cover the slim figure she saw in the mirror. She shivered a little, fighting the little wave of depression.

5

She closed her eyes tight for a moment, then gave herself a little shake. Quickly she got dressed in the familiar camelhair suit. 'That's what I get,' she muttered to herself as she moved briskly into the kitchen, 'for letting a little sunshine go to my head!'

By the time she locked the front door behind her and hurried to the bus stop on the corner, she was able to look at the mood dispassionately and recognize it for what it was. 'I am twenty-six years old,' she recited under her breath as she walked along, heels tapping on the sidewalk, 'probably the only virgin of that age left in the city of Seattle. Perhaps the world.'

Now, finally, she could smile at herself as she joined the usual morning crowd at the bus stop.

It had turned out to be even warmer than the harried and misunderstood weatherman had predicted, and by the time Katherine stepped inside the building at five to nine her wool jacket already felt too warm.

She saw Teresa Rugetti standing toward the front of a crowded elevator. She held it open for Katherine and beckoned her forward. Katherine quickened her step and got inside.

'Thanks, Teresa,' she said. She glanced at her friend's cotton dress, sleeveless and low cut. 'I wish I'd had the sense to wear something cooler,' she said as they moved slowly upward.

'Don't worry,' said Teresa with a snort of disgust, 'they've already turned on the air-conditioning. Sixty-five degrees out and they think it's a heat-wave!'

Her voice carried, and she glanced around the elevator at the tense, bored faces of the lawyers, accountants and secretaries who worked in the building. She seemed to be seeking confirmation of her opinion of all the higher powers that made such momentous decisions as when to turn on the air-conditioning.

Katherine smiled. Although Teresa was her exact opposite in looks, temperament, life-style and background, there was something warm and appealing about the volatile Italian girl that had drawn Katherine in the two years they had worked together.

They stepped out of the elevator into the plushly carpeted foyer of the prestigious law firm where they both worked. Immediately they were hit with a blast of cold air. Teresa hugged her arms and shivered.

'See? What'd I tell you?'

'You'll be glad of it this afternoon when the sun hits our side of the building. Don't you have a sweater?'

'Who, me? I'm lucky to have a dress. You know what that rat did over the weekend?'

Teresa launched into a long and vivid description of the most recent escapade of her irresponsible husband, Tony. It was the same old story—a lost job, gambling debts, drink, the suspicion of another woman.

'And then he has the nerve to criticise my cooking!' she ended her recital as they reached their desks. 'So I picked up the salad and dumped it on his head.'

'Oh, Teresa,' Katherine gasped, grinning in spite of herself, 'you didn't!'

'I sure did.' Teresa was triumphant. She sat at her desk and removed the cover from her typewriter. 'I wish it had been the hot spaghetti!'

Katherine took off her jacket and hung it neatly over the back of her chair. 'What did Tony do then?' she asked.

'Well, for a minute I thought he was going to sock me. He just stood there with Caesar salad in his hair and sticking to his clothes, his fist raised. Then I started to pick the salad off him and eat it. Then we both started to giggle.'

'So it ended up okay?'

'Oh, sure. Same place it always does—in bed.' Teresa sighed as she rolled a clean sheet of paper into her typewriter. 'I can't help it. I know he's no good, but I love him.'

The keys of her typewriter began to clack. Katherine turned her head and reached down into her bottom drawer so no one would see her face. She bit her lip to ward off the longing that rose up in her. She tried to reason with herself, to remind herself that she wouldn't trade her calm, orderly life for the perpetual three-ring circus at Teresa's house for anything.

'How was your weekend?' Teresa called to her over the noise of her typewriter keys. 'Do anything exciting?'

'Nothing spectacular.' Katherine never ceased to wonder how Teresa could type and carry on a conversation at the same time. 'I just went over to Bainbridge Island, to my brother's place.'

The typewriter halted abruptly. 'I don't get you,' Teresa remarked, staring. 'A good-looking girl like you, a boss eating out of your hand, and you spend your weekends at your brother's or spraying your roses, or . . .' She shook her head then resumed her typing. 'I give up. I don't get you.'

'Don't try, then,' Katherine said lightly. 'To each his own, you know.' It was an old familiar argument.

Teresa snorted. To her, any woman was mentally retarded who didn't have a man to fight with and love.

Katherine put on her glasses and turned to her work. Her boss, Jim Hawkins, had recently filed an anti-trust suit in federal court against four timber companies in Western Washington on behalf of a paper manufacturing company. In the two years Katherine had worked at the Powell, Cable & Hawkins law firm she had become adept at handling the voluminous correspondence, legal pleadings and documents involved in anti-trust cases, and she had just started organising the files on this one last week. She knew that the earlier she imposed order on the reams of paper generated by these cases, the easier it was going to be to find things later on, as the case progressed.

She worked steadily drawing up a list of the files she would need to set up for the documents already in hand. By ten o'clock the sun had crept around to the window behind her. She could feel its warmth on her back through the thin silk of her blouse. Her mind began to wander. She leaned forward on her desk, chin in hand, staring into space, the files forgotten. Teresa's comment on her weekend, familiar though it was, had disturbed her. Maybe, she thought, it's the sunshine. It seemed to make her restless, vaguely dissatisfied.

No, she said to herself firmly, in that direction lies chaos. She could handle the passing mood; she had in the past. There could be no order without sticking to a decision rationally made, and she wanted an orderly life. When she was tempted like this, she reasoned, there was no point in going back and re-examining the decision, made seven years ago when she was nineteen, that men and women seemed to be natural enemies, that there was too much heartache involved in love.

At bottom, she knew, was the stark fact that after what had happened all those years ago she didn't dare trust herself to fall in love, to take that chance. She had been so devastated then, so full of self-condemnation and self-hatred for the terrible mistakes she had made, that she had sworn she would never allow that kind of relationship to mess up her life again.

She glanced at Teresa, busily typing away, her fingers flying, a little half-smile on her face, and once again felt a little stab of envy. Teresa's life was just that kind of chaos Katherine wanted to avoid. She knew she would never survive living in a state of perpetual conflict, no matter how much she loved a man.

She thought of her brother and his wife. They had a calm, easygoing relationship and seemed to be content with each other. But there was no spark. She shook herself a little and sat up straight, the incongruity of her train of thought striking her forcefully. She didn't want chaos and she didn't want contentment. What did she want?

She decided not to explore that fruitless avenue and returned to her work. She reached for the pile of papers in the wooden tray on the corner of her desk, lifting up the glass paperweight, an object so familiar she ordinarily paid no attention to it. This morning, however, she held it up in front of her and tipped it from side to side.

A little storm of artificial snowflakes immediately filled the glass dome, showering down on the tiny figures of a boy and girl pulling sleds. Years ago, when she had burned Luke's short letters, torn up his pictures and thrown out the few dried flowers and small trinkets he had given her, she somehow couldn't part with the paperweight.

'Are you dreaming of a white Christmas on our one day of sunshine, Katherine?'

She looked up. Her boss, Jim Hawkins, stood at her desk, a pile of papers in his hands. He was smiling down at her.

Lightly she dropped the paperweight back in the tray and ran a hand over her smooth golden hair. She looked up at Jim with a smile.

'It's the sun, Jim. We're not used to it. It affects the brain.'

His clear blue eyes were gentle. He set the papers down on her desk, reached across and laid a hand lightly on her arm.

'Nothing could affect your brain, Katherine,' he said in a low voice.

'Little do you know,' she rejoined. His frequent

displays of affection for her made her uncomfortable. She could feel Teresa's eyes boring into them,
her typewriter silent. 'I see you've brought me a
present,' she said, gesturing towards the pile of
papers.

Jim sighed and withdrew his hand. 'I'm afraid it's
going to be one of *those* cases,' he said, smiling
ruefully. 'You know, on and on, drowning in
paper, ten copies of everything, last-minute filings
in court. You're familiar with the scenario by now.'

She stood up and scooped the papers into her
arms, setting them down on top of the filing cabinet
behind her desk.

'All in a day's work, sir,' she called over her
shoulder. 'What are these?'

'First wave discovery documents from one of the
defendants. If you'll take care of those, I'll get on
with dictating our first request for admissions of
facts. It has to be served and filed by Friday, so I'm
trying to get an early start.'

'What?' Katherine asked playfully. She raised
her eyebrows and opened her eyes wide. 'And spoil
our record of mad dashes to serve and file at
four-thirty Friday afternoon?'

He chuckled. 'Okay, okay, I guess I deserve that!
You know by now that procrastination is a lawyer's
occupational hazard.' He started to leave, then
turned back and leaned over her desk. 'How about
lunch today?' he said, his voice low.

Katherine couldn't hold back the fleeting frown
that crossed her forehead. In the two years she had
worked for Jim Hawkins she had come to like him
very much as a friend and employer. Gradually, as

the months of close association passed by, she could see his liking for her turn into something more serious. A lawyer and his secretary form a close relationship in their work together, as close as doctor and nurse. If she is good at her job, she becomes her boss's right arm, an extension of his working self.

'Oh, Jim,' she said, 'I don't think so. I'm afraid people will talk if we're seen together too much.'

'Who cares?'

'I care,' she said lightly. She smiled to take the sting out of her words. 'I have to work with these girls.'

'You're a hard woman,' he said playfully, and left.

Katherine had realised and accepted from the beginning of her work as a legal secretary that her main function was to make her boss's work easier. She saw that there was no great future for her, no place to go, no upward mobility in working for a professional man. But the work was interesting, the pay excellent, the physical surroundings pleasant.

Jim Hawkins' growing affection for her was flattering. He was quite a bit older than she, close to forty, she would guess. He was lonely, she knew. He and his wife had been divorced for several years and she lived in Los Angeles with their two children.

He was a good-looking man, with a trim slender build, smooth light brown hair and really beautiful blue eyes. He dressed well, took her to the best restaurants, the theatre, concerts, but she kept him at a distance. There was no spark for her in their rare tepid kisses, nor did she look for one or want one. It was just a pleasant relationship, on the job and off, but she was afraid Jim was getting more serious all the time, and she didn't want to hurt him.

She had told him often enough she didn't love him and never could, but he seemed to derive so much pleasure from her company that he obeyed her rules to the letter and never forced more on her than she was willing to take.

She worked steadily setting up the files for the paper case with total concentration for over an hour.

'Are you coming?' Teresa was standing at her desk. 'Come on, it's time for a break.'

Katherine took off her glasses and blinked. 'Oh, sure,' she said. 'I'm at a stopping point.'

'I've got some hot gossip,' Teresa confided in a low voice as they walked down the carpeted corridor to the coffee room.

'Oh, Teresa, not another office romance!' Katherine groaned in mock dismay.

Teresa glared at her and shook her black curls angrily. 'No, Miss Smarty, not another office romance. You and Jim Hawkins take care of that department.'

'Oh, come on,' said Katherine, annoyed, 'that's no romance and you know it.'

Teresa eyed her knowingly, nodding her head. 'Oh no? I see the way he looks at you.'

'Don't be silly. Come on, what's the gossip?'

They poured themselves cups of coffee from the

pots on the counter and sat down at one of the small round tables.

'Well, it has to do with you, actually.' Teresa lowered her voice and leaned across the table, bracelets jangling on the red formica top. 'You're getting a co-counsel from New York on the paper case.'

Katherine took a sip of coffee and cocked her head to one side. 'So? We usually do when the local client is a subsidiary. The parent company always sends out its own lawyer to keep an eye on things.'

'Yes, but I heard this one is going to try the case himself.' Teresa sat back in her chair and grinned triumphantly.

Katherine frowned. 'I don't understand. Why? We always try our own cases. What about Jim?'

'What I heard is that this guy they're sending out is a real hot shot—great courtroom acrobat.'

Katherine tipped her coffee from side to side in the white plastic cup, then quickly drained it and stood up abruptly. She didn't want Teresa to see how disturbed she was.

'It's only gossip, Teresa. You hear these things and half the time they aren't true.'

Teresa opened her mouth to reply when Sharon, the receptionist, poked her head around the corner of the room.

'Katherine,' she called, 'Jim wants you to phone him in his office.' She stepped inside and beckoned frantically. 'Wait until you see what he's got in there with him! What a dreamboat!'

'Who is it?' Katherine asked as they walked out together.

'Some guy just got in from New York.' Sharon hissed. 'Wait'll you see him!' She rolled her eyes. 'About six feet three, shoulders out to here, no hips, black hair, dreamy dark eyes, and mean-looking.'

So Teresa's gossip was true after all, Katherine thought as she hurried to her desk. Poor Jim! He wasn't going to like that. Just as she picked up the telephone to call him, he came around the corner of the hallway and walked towards her. His expression was blank, but as he moved closer she could see the little worry lines on his forehead.

He took her arm and led her into the vacant office next door, shutting the door behind him.

'Listen,' he said, 'this has got to be quick. The client has sent out their own lawyer to try the case.' He raised a hand to silence her protest. 'We'll work it out, don't worry.' His tone was grim, determined. 'But we've got to handle it with kid gloves.' He glanced at his watch. 'I'm due at a meeting in two minutes at the Donahue firm—be back in about an hour. Will you go into my office and fill this guy in on the case? You know, the discovery so far, motions made on both sides, the judge's opinions, the case law I've put together. Also get him a copy of the Local Rules for Federal Court. I've got to run. Just take care of him.'

He reached for the door. 'I'm sorry, Katherine, I hate to stick you with this. The guy's supposed to be brilliant, but he's pretty abrupt. Be nice to him, now, and I'll see if we can't get rid of him in time.'

'No problem, Jim,' she said, collecting herself. 'I'll do what I can.'

'Good girl!' He grinned. 'I knew I could count on you.' He turned back once more. 'By the way, his name is Dillon—Luke Dillon. Take him some coffee or something.'

Then he was gone. Katherine's head began to whirl. She put a hand to her throat. She felt so dizzy she had to sit down. She groped her way to a chair and sank into it.

Luke Dillon! 'No,' she whispered to herself. 'It couldn't be!' Her heart was pounding so hard she could hear it.

She propped her head up with her hand, her elbow resting on the desk in front of her, and tried to collect her thoughts. Gradually she grew calmer, the throbbing heartbeats subsiding.

Number one, she thought, it probably isn't the same one. Sure, my Luke Dillon was going to law school, but it's not that unusual a name. Number two, even if it is, it's been almost ten years. We were just kids. And number three, if he's a successful New York trial lawyer, what happened years ago has probably faded from his mind. Surely that would be the least of his concerns.

He was waiting for her now in Jim's office. Once again her heart began to pound. She stood up, smoothed her skirt and ran a hand over her hair to see that it was securely pinned. She stopped at her desk on the way to pick up her glasses, more a defence mechanism than necessary for vision.

She could sense Teresa's eyes boring into her and gave her a little grin and shrug as she passed by. As she turned the corner her eye was caught by the glass paperweight on her desk as a shaft of sunlight hit it, and her heart sank. She prayed it would be a different Luke Dillon.

At the door to Jim's office, she hesitated for a moment, then quietly opened it and stepped inside.

He was standing with his back to her looking out at the busy harbour of Puget Sound below. The ferry to Bainbridge Island was halfway across. There were small fishing boats, sailboats, and a tug chugging out to meet a freighter just coming in from Alaska. On the other side of the Sound, the Olympic Mountains rose, snow-capped, in the distant blue of the clear sky.

Katherine knew him at once. There was no mistaking that tall figure with the broad shoulders and slim hips, the shock of black crisp hair, so unruly then, styled to perfection now.

Even in his beautifully tailored charcoal grey suit that hung expertly on his lean, hard body, a complete contrast to the faded jeans and sloppy sweaters he wore as a boy, Katherine would have known him anywhere.

She had to summon up all her strength of will to do it, but eventually she managed to speak, still nursing the dim hope that it wasn't he, or that if it was he wouldn't recognise her.

'Mr Dillon,' she said in a clear voice that surprised her with its calm, businesslike tone, 'I'm Katherine Croft, Jim Hawkins' secretary.'

He turned around slowly and their eyes met briefly. Did she imagine it, or did his eyes open a little wider at the sight of her? For it was, indeed, the Luke Dillon of her past. Older, leaner, more confident appearing and urbane, but with the same black hair, the same deeply-set brown eyes with the same unruly gleam of wildness in them, the same hawklike nose and determined chin.

He crossed the width of the office in leisurely steps, his left hand in his trousers pocket. He skirted the desk deftly and held out his right hand.

'How do you do. I'm Luke Dillon.'

His voice was deep and controlled, the tone pleasant but businesslike, giving away nothing. There was not a flicker of recognition in those hooded eyes. She took his hand. He shook it briefly, his grip strong and warm, then released it.

'Jim—Mr Hawkins—asked me to show you the documents in the paper case,' she said evenly. She repressed a faint flicker of disappointment that he hadn't even remembered her. A vague feeling of regret passed through her mind at the years of guilty penance she had spent over him.

'Yes,' he replied, 'and since I'll be here for some time, I'd like to use an office if you have one to spare.'

'I think that can be arranged,' she said coolly. 'There's one right next to me that's empty. In fact, I keep some of the files in there.'

He followed her down the corridor and she felt his eyes on her as she walked in front of him. She led him to the empty office. As they walked past the desks of the other secretaries, she could see them staring, their looks full of approval and envy.

Katherine showed Luke Dillon the file cabinet behind her desk, the drawer neatly labelled 'Paper Case.'

'I keep all the correspondence, pleadings and

notes in here,' she said, opening the drawer. 'All our correspondence is kept chronologically and I index each volume of pleadings, which are also chronological.'

He was standing at her right and slightly behind her, intent on the contents of the drawer. He was so close she could hear his even breath, smell the light aftershave and feel the rough wool material of his jacket as it brushed the thin silk of her blouse when he reached for the pleading file.

She kept her eyes straight ahead, both hands on the open file drawer, as he examined the file. His attention was totally concentrated on the business at hand.

'I see you don't separate discovery pleadings from motions,' he said at last.

'No,' she said. 'I've found it's easier to locate a pleading when they're filed strictly by date.'

She glanced at him out of the corner of her eye. He nodded, his face expressionless. He replaced the file in the drawer.

'I'd like to take a look at the documents you've gathered so far.'

'This way,' she said. She led him to the empty office next door.

He glanced through the folders swiftly while she waited, pausing occasionally for a closer look. Finally he set them down on the desk.

'I can use this office?' he asked, seating himself at the desk.

'Yes, I'm sure it will be all right.'

'Then I'll just start studying the case. Perhaps you'd bring me the pleading file. I want to review the original complaint and defendants' answers.'

'Certainly, Mr Dillon,' she said crisply. 'Anything else? How about a cup of coffee?'

'Yes, thank you,' he murmured absently, totally engrossed now in the papers spread out before him. 'Black, please.'

When she brought him the file and his coffee, he neither looked up nor spoke. His dark head was bent over the desk, his eyes narrowed in concentration.

As she set the coffee down, Katherine glanced at him from beneath her lowered eyelashes. His arms lay quietly on the table as he read. It was so still in the room she could hear the ticking of his watch.

Katherine was not a fanciful or overly-imaginative woman. She felt she was level-headed, sensible, practical. Yet, as she stood there, her hand still on the coffee cup, she experienced an odd sensation of paralysis, as though she were rooted to the spot and couldn't move.

She found herself staring at the ticking watch, just visible below the crisp white cuff of his shirt. It was a thin gold watch with a leather strap, buckled just above the prominent bone of his wrist. The silky black hairs of his wrist and the shape of his hand brought back a flood of recollection from the past.

Then, suddenly, she became aware that something indefinable was passing between them, like an electric current, and that even though he still hadn't so much as flicked an eye in her direction or acknowledged her presence in any way, he was as intensely physically aware of her as she was of him.

Then he looked up at her. She caught her breath, and the spell was broken. He raised one heavy black eyebrow and gave her a curious look.

'Thank you, Miss Croft. You've been very helpful.'

She straightened up, collected herself and nodded briefly at him.

'I'll be right next door at my desk if you need me for anything.'

She turned and left the room, shutting the door quietly behind her. She went to her desk, sat down and busied herself with shuffling some papers mindlessly about. Teresa was watching her.

'Now, that is some man,' she whispered loudly. 'Wow!'

Katherine ignored her. She felt as though a yawning chasm had opened at her feet and that if she didn't hang on to her calm, safe, orderly world, she would be drawn into some dangerous whirlpool of emotion she was not prepared to deal with.

'He's only a mortal, Teresa,' she said dryly, and started to type up Jim's tape.

CHAPTER TWO

THE next day dawned bright and sunny again, and Katherine decided to wear the new blue suit. She arranged her early morning schedule so that she would have fifteen minutes in her small rose garden to prune off the spent blooms and check for signs of disease.

While she was in the garden bemoaning the incipient black spot on the Peace and making a mental note to spray this evening, the sun beat down so warmly on her back that she decided to dash inside the house to change her blouse from the long-sleeved pale blue silk to a crisp sleeveless white piqué vest. The neckline seemed a little low to her, even with the jacket on, so she quickly tied a blue and white scarf around her neck and tucked it into the vee of the bosom.

She had spent a sleepless night, tossing and turning, going over her meeting with Luke Dillon after all these years. She couldn't help being a little provoked that he either hadn't recognised her or had chosen not to acknowledge their old connection, but by morning, her good sense had prevailed.

Katherine's major goal in life was to lead a quiet, orderly existence. This being the case, she reasoned to herself as she stared out the bus window on her way downtown, Luke's coolness fitted into her plans exactly.

She rode up on the elevator with Irene Connors, the managing partner's secretary. Irene was a tall blonde who affected dramatic—and expensive—clothes. There had been some speculation in the coffee room as to the provider of Irene's vast wardrobe, and the current consensus was that old man Powell was the lucky man.

This morning she was wearing a filmy voile print splashed with pale violets and light green leaves. The scooped neckline was cut low with a ruffle around it.

'That's a beautiful dress, Irene,' Katherine remarked. Secretly she thought it far too dressy for office wear, but then decided she probably had a date after work.

'Thanks,' Irene replied, smoothing her elaborately coiled and stiffly sprayed coiffure. 'I was glad to see the sunshine again this morning so I could wear it to the party.'

As they got off the elevator, Irene put a hand on Katherine's arm and bent down to whisper to her: 'Say, who's the new man in the office next to you? One of ours?'

Katherine explained briefly who Luke Dillon was.

'Is he married?'

'No,' Katherine said without thinking.

As she made her way to her desk she wondered what had made her say that. Why was she so sure Luke Dillon wasn't married? She was annoyed at Irene for even bringing up the subject.

Teresa was already at her desk.

'Hey,' she called, 'why so glum?'

Katherine gave her a quick glance as she sat down and uncovered her typewriter.

'Oh, I found some black spot on my Peace rose this morning,' she replied lightly.

Teresa had crossed over and was standing in front of Katherine's desk. Katherine glanced up at her. Her eyes widened as she saw the dress Teresa was wearing, shocking pink polished cotton with a tight bodice and flaring skirt.

'Hey,' Katherine exclaimed, 'what goes on? The sun comes out and everyone goes berserk! First Irene, now you. I suppose next Mr Powell will show up in his Bermuda shorts.'

Teresa twirled on her high-heeled pink sandals. 'Like it?' she asked, pleased with herself. 'Tony says it makes me look like an Italian Bo Derek.'

'Well, yes,' Katherine faltered, 'but isn't it a little—well, dressy for work?'

Teresa's eyes widened as she glanced at Katherine's blue linen jacket and silk scarf.

'Are you going to the party dressed like that?' she exclaimed.

'What party?' Katherine asked, bewildered.

'What party? Why, the office party we've only been planning for a month. What party!' Teresa flounced back to her desk and flopped down on her chair. 'Honestly, Katherine, you are so *out* of it. Where have you been?'

Then Katherine remembered. The firm had recently remodelled and expanded its office, and today, June the twenty-seventh, was holding an open house for staff and clients.

She glanced down at her tailored attire. 'Oh,

well,' she said, shrugging, 'no one will notice.'

Teresa snorted and muttered something to herself about old maids and middle-aged virgins as her fingers flew over her typewriter keys. Katherine smiled and turned her mind to her work.

As she had passed by the office next door she had noticed that every available surface in the room was strewn with papers, but that Luke Dillon wasn't there. Now she got up and went to the door. She peered inside and groaned inwardly at the thought of how long it had taken her to organise all those documents into neat categories.

The telephone on her desk began to ring and she ran to answer it.

'Yes? Katherine Croft speaking.'

'Good morning,' came a familiar voice.

'Good morning, Jim.'

'Would you please come to my office?'

'Right away.' She grabbed pencil and notebook from her desk.

Jim was alone in his office. He looked glum, but when he saw her his face brightened. He removed his feet from the top of his desk and stood up.

'Come in, Katherine. Shut the door.' She did so.

They both sat down. Jim leaned forward, elbows on the desk, his chin in his hands, a crooked grin on his face.

Looking across the desk at him, her pencil poised for instructions, she thought of how much she liked him, how comfortable she felt with him. She even wished she could love him at times, or could respond to him without loving him. He would marry her in a minute, she knew, with the slightest en-

couragement on her part. She would be safe, secure, perhaps have a family. Then she dismissed
such thoughts as he started to speak to her.

'Well, it's confirmed by the client,' he said. He
grabbed a pencil and began tapping it on the desk,
staring down at it. He looked at her. 'Luke Dillon is
now in charge of the paper case.'

'It's not fair,' she said, bristling. 'It's *your* case.'

'No,' he corrected her, 'it's the client's case.'

She thought a moment, then asked: 'Does that
mean we're off the case?' She thought of the jumble
of papers in Luke's office and began to hope that
now someone else would have to straighten out that
mess.

'Not entirely.' He eyed her warily. 'I'll be doing
the discovery, taking depositions, inspecting and
producing documents. He'll determine the course
we take, prepare and argue the motions, do the
negotiating with defendants.'

'I see,' she said drily. 'He'll just do all the interesting parts.'

He chuckled. 'Something like that.' His clear
blue eyes softened as he gazed at her. 'It's almost
worth it, Katherine, to see how loyal you are to my
interests. With you in my corner, he can have the
case.'

Katherine lowered her eyes. She always tried to
avoid any show of emotional attachment to him.

He cleared his throat and sat back in his chair.
'However, since we're all on the client's side in the
end, I hope you'll give Luke every co-operation.'

'What do you mean?' she asked, suddenly suspicious.

'Well, I'll be travelling to depositions for the most part, and he'll be here. You're familiar with the case. So, in effect, you'll be his secretary.'

Katherine was stunned into silence. The last thing she wanted was to work closely with Luke Dillon.

'Whose idea was that?' she asked finally.

Jim hesitated. Instead of answering her directly, he asked gently, 'You don't like him, for some reason. Yet you don't even know him. Why?'

'I don't dislike him. I just don't like to see you eased off your own case.'

He stood up. 'Come on, Katherine, be a good sport. He's a fine lawyer, one of the best. You know anti-trust cases rarely come to trial. We'll probably settle before long.'

She rose to go. 'I sincerely hope so!'

During the day the main topic of conversation in the coffee room was the party. By late afternoon a bar had been set up in the large conference room, and Sharon, the receptionist-cum-hostess, was busy at the stove in the coffee room preparing hors d'oeuvres and arranging nuts, chips and dips in various bowls.

Luke Dillon hadn't shown up in the office at all that day, and Katherine had firmly closed her mind to the mess in his office. Jim had other cases, and she worked on those all day tidying up loose ends and arranging his hotel and plane reservations for San Francisco. He left right after noon.

The office was officially closed for business at five o'clock. Katherine had been the butt all day of comments about her appearance, and by five she was beginning to get angry.

'Why don't you at least take your jacket off?' Teresa hissed at her. 'You make everyone uncomfortable.'

'Oh, come on, Teresa. The men have jackets on,' she replied.

'They won't for long,' Irene purred. She already had a drink in her hand and was leering over the rim of her glass. 'The air-conditioning goes off at five, and they'll begin to peel down to their shirtsleeves before long.'

It *was* getting warm, Katherine thought to herself uncomfortably, as the guests began to trickle in and the room to fill up. The drinks were flowing freely by six o'clock, the crowd getting noisier, and someone had brought a radio which was blaring dance music.

As she got warmer and warmer in her jacket, Katherine began to think the best thing she could do was slip out quietly and go home.

As she made her way to the door, Teresa grabbed her arm and thrust a drink in her hand. 'Here,' she said, 'this'll cool you off.' Katherine sipped at it. It did taste refreshing. She glanced around the room.

In a corner Irene Connors and old man Powell were trying to dance. Soon other couples joined them. Someone dimmed the lights, and Katherine stared in amazement at the unexpected behaviour of her co-workers. She finished the drink Teresa had given her and someone handed her another one. She found that the drink softened the impact of the scene, made the noise less deafening, the strange contortions of the dancers less objectionable.

Teresa was at her side again, looking at her disgustedly. 'Come into the ladies' room for a minute,' she said at last.

'Why?' Katherine asked.

'Never mind, just come along,' and she pulled her inside. 'Now,' Teresa said firmly, blinking at the sudden glare, 'take that jacket off.' Katherine stared at her. 'Come on, take it off, party pooper!'

Suddenly Katherine began to giggle. Teresa was right—she was being silly. She knew it was probably the drink, the noise, the music, but suddenly she thought to herself, why not just relax and try to enjoy myself?

She slipped off her jacket and hung it on the clothes rack. Teresa eyed her appraisingly. 'Okay, that's better. The vest fits well, shows you have a figure after all. Now, take off the scarf and unpin your hair and we'll be in business. And take off those glasses. I know you don't need them.'

Meekly, Katherine obeyed. Off came the scarf and glasses, down came the hair. She spread her arms wide and stood before Teresa.

'Now, are you satisfied?'

Teresa only stared, then gave a low appreciative whistle.

'I can't believe it,' she said finally. 'You're a different person. I'm glad Tony's not here.'

Katherine turned and looked in the mirror. The honey-coloured hair hung loosely to her shoulders. Her arms and throat were bare, and the plunging vee and close-fitting bodice of the vest showed off her well-rounded figure to full advantage.

In spite of her growing trepidation, Katherine was quite pleased with her appearance. The severe, efficient secretary had vanished along with the glasses, hairpins, scarf and jacket. She looked, she decided, quite seductive.

'Come on,' Teresa called. 'I can hardly wait for the others to see you!'

Katherine hesitated. It was one thing to look seductive in the safety of the ladies' room, but quite another to display it in front of the whole office.

Teresa was pulling at her, and the next thing she knew she was back in the coffee room. As her eyes became accustomed to the dimmer light she could see that the men had indeed shed their jackets.

She took a quick swallow of her drink to muster the courage to walk into that roomful of people. Teresa had vanished, no doubt to herald her grand entrance, Katherine thought.

Then her head cleared suddenly, and she knew she couldn't do it. She felt immeasurably detached from the noisy, milling crowd. Irene was up on the table now, doing a drunken seductive dance, cheered on by the younger lawyers. Katherine knew that she would a hundred, a thousand times rather be in her garden spraying her roses than have any part of such a party.

She turned back towards the rest room, stumbling in her haste. As she started to trip a firm hand was clamped on her bare arm, steadying her.

'Not too drunk to walk already, are you, Miss Croft?' came a deep masculine voice.

Katherine looked up angrily into the mocking dark eyes of Luke Dillon. His thin mouth was twisted into a derisive smile, the heavy eyebrows raised in amusement.

'I am not drunk,' she said icily, 'merely in a hurry.'

'Why?'

'To get out of here,' she snapped.

'What for?'

By now he had guided her firmly out of the noisy room and she found herself facing him at the bank of elevators by the reception room.

'Because,' she said distinctly, 'I want to go home to spray my roses.'

He punched the elevator button. 'You can't spray you roses now.'

'Why not?'

He shrugged. 'It's dark already.'

The elevator appeared, disgorged its passengers, and he propelled her inside. They started down.

It all happened so fast that Katherine hadn't had time to think. Luke's large hand still gripped her bare arm. She glanced sideways at him. He was looking straight ahead, whistling softly under his breath.

It was indeed dark outside. Out on the sidewalk in front of the building, Katherine realised she had left her jacket in the rest-room. She did still have her handbag, however.

'Goodnight,' she muttered, and tried to pull herself free from his iron grip.

'Where are you going?' he asked.

'To get my bus. I'm going home, remember?'

'I'll drive you.'

Katherine's fuzzy mind began to function normally at last. Quickly she assessed the situation. He obviously had not recognised her. She was using her married name now. He had known her as Katherine Evans, and had always called her Katie. Her appearance had certainly changed in ten years, especially with the severe image she projected in the office.

'All right,' she said finally. Since they'd be working closely together, she decided, they might as well be on good terms.

He drove expertly and quickly. The rush hour traffic had thinned by now, and in fifteen minutes they pulled up in front of her small grey cottage on Queen Anne Hill.

'Thanks for the ride,' she said. On the way out their only conversation had consisted of her directions and his swearing at Seattle's terrible drivers, who consistently did the unexpected, 'I'll see you tomorrow.'

'Would you like some supper?' he asked. 'I'm starving!'

She turned to look at him, unsure of what he meant. Was he inviting her out to dinner? The street light on the corner gleamed through the front windshield, lighting his features. She gasped silently, inwardly, as she met his gaze and saw the same solemn look she had loved so in the Luke Dillon of so many years ago. Her heart began to pound.

'Would you like to come in?' she said in a low

voice. 'I can fix us something.'

The dark eyes gleamed. 'I thought you'd never ask.'

She unlocked the front door and stepped inside, sensing him right behind her. She reached out to flick on the living room light when she felt his firm grip once again on her bare arm, restraining her. She heard the door click shut.

She closed her eyes. Her mind told her to move, to cry out, to break this spell his presence had cast on her, but she was physically unable to do so. Not only had she had more to drink this evening than she was used to, but Luke's presence in her house had immobilised her defences.

She could feel the rough material of his jacket against her arm as he slowly turned her around to face him.

I must stop this now, she warned herself, before it gets out of hand. She could feel her pleasant life slipping out of her grasp, her hard-won security shattering unless she moved away from this man, right now. But she couldn't. Because of the past, Luke Dillon had become more an irresistible force in her life than a mere man, and she was helpless under his touch.

The porch light shone dimly into the room. His face was in the shadows and she couldn't read its expression. He raised a hand and placed it lightly on her cheek. It was warm, strong, and seemed to contain her being. She closed her eyes.

'You're very beautiful,' he said in a low voice. His hand moved to her throat.

'I think I'd better . . .' she began, struggling

against the rising tide of desire that threatened to engulf her.

Then his mouth was on hers, cutting off her words. She melted under his kiss, tasting once again the familiar sweetness of Luke Dillon's lips burning into her own. His mouth played with hers, rubbing against it softly, then barely touching it, then, forcing her lips open, clamped on it possessively as if he would consume her.

She groaned as his arms went around her, crushing her to him. It was as though all the passion she had suppressed through the long years was suddenly unleashed, and she strained eagerly against him. Without releasing the pressure of his mouth on hers, he deftly slipped of his jacket. When his arms were free he put his hands on her throat again, then lowered them to the vee of her blouse. He slowly undid the buttons and pushed it open.

Then his kiss became even more insistent, pushing her head back so that she would have fallen backwards if his strong hand hadn't come around to support the back of her neck. She felt his other hand on her breast, the flimsy lace of her bra moving sensually over her bare skin as his fingers explored relentlessly. He lifted the gauzy material over the full straining breast and brought his mouth down to kiss the hardening tip, all the while his hand moulding the soft white fullness around it.

Every gesture came so naturally, so familiarly, as if they were replaying a scene they both knew by heart. Katherine reached out to him and began to unbutton his thin shirt, her hands eagerly exploring the bare skin underneath. She shuddered at the feel of the hard muscles of his chest and back.

She lifted her head and kissed his throat, his chest. He still held her at the back of the neck with one hand, the other cupping her bare breast, his thumb making circles across the taut nipple. She groaned again as the sensation pierced her whole body with aching desire. Luke put his cheek against hers and began to whisper in her ear.

'Do you like that, Katie? Tell me how much you like it. You always used to.'

She stiffened. Katie, she thought. He called me Katie!

Slowly she drew back and stared up at him, her eyes wide with sudden apprehension. By the glow of the street light she could see the sardonic grin on his face, the wild gleam in his dark eyes, now full of total recognition.

At that moment his hands left her body abruptly and he stepped back from her. She stared at him, pulling her skimpy blouse together to cover her nakedness. He was lazily buttoning his shirt, the grin still on his face, his eyes now burning with hatred.

'You knew!' she breathed. 'You knew all along who I was!'

Casually he lit a cigarette. In the sudden flare of the match she could clearly see his tousled dark hair falling over his forehead, the thick black eyelashes brushing his cheekbones. He shook out the match.

'Of course I knew,' he said in a low venomous voice. 'Did you think I'd ever forget? I've been carrying around a load of poison in my gut for almost ten years waiting for a chance to get rid of it. Now I have,' he added with satisfaction.

Katherine straightened her clothing and smoothed back her hair. She was badly shaken and bewildered, unsure of how to meet the cruel arrogance of this man.

Then, slowly, anger began to rise in her like a volcano about to erupt. She wanted to slap that smug face, to claw it with her fingernails, to draw blood. With an enormous effort she fought the fury down.

'Then I guess the score is settled at last,' she said evenly through clenched teeth. 'We're quits now.'

Luke reached down and stabbed his cigarette out viciously in the ashtray on the coffee table.

'Yes,' he said at last, 'I guess we are.'

He picked up his coat off the floor where it had fallen, slung it over one shoulder and turned to go.

I knew I'd hurt you,' she said in a low voice, 'but I never realised how much until now, that you could do this to me. I hope it was worth it.'

He whirled around, grabbed her by the shoulders and shook her roughly.

'Yes,' he breathed angrily, 'you hurt me. I worshipped you! I never once—not once—doubted that you would wait for me. My trust in you was absolute. And the first thing you do, while I'm slaving my tail off trying to play football, go to school and hold down a job, is fall for the first guy that comes along with a fancy car and money to spend!'

His words hit her like a spray of bullets. She put her hands over her face and turned away. She knew she had been wrong, years ago, but for Luke to have carried this terrible load of bitterness and hatred for so long was beyond belief.

'Luke,' she whispered, 'we were children!'

'Oh, come on,' he growled. 'Children? Hardly that!'

She knew him too well to think there was any hope of reasoning with him. He had a will of iron.

'All right,' she said, calmer now. 'As we agreed, now we're even. I hope you enjoyed your revenge.'

He raised one heavy eyebrow. 'Oh, I did, Katherine, I did.' His eyes swept her from head to toe. 'Obviously, so did you.'

She reddened, recalling the feel of his hands on her bare skin and her passionate response. She raised her chin.

'That fact should add to your pleasure.'

He grinned broadly, wickedly. There would be no shaming this man, Katherine thought, and in spite of her hurt and humiliation, she still felt the impulse to reach out to him, as she would have the old Luke, the vulnerable Luke, to cradle the dark head in her arms, against her breast, to smooth back the crisp hairs and kiss the lean cheek. But the old Luke had vanished into this cruel, hard-eyed stranger who only wanted to hurt her.

She watched him in the dimness as he put on his jacket and walked away. At the door he turned back to her.

'By the way, what ever happened to Brian Croft, my successor?' His tone was cutting.

Like a knife in her heart, the old wound opened

and she felt as though her life's blood was draining out of her body.

'That's a long story,' she said at last, her voice dead.

Again he raised one eyebrow. 'I see. Another victim? You've chalked up quite a track record. Who's next? Jim Hawkins? He seems willing enough, a good prospect. Maybe I'd better warn him about you.'

'You do that, Luke,' she said dully.

He opened the door. 'Goodnight, Katherine.'

'Goodbye, Luke,' she said. She closed and locked the door after him.

For a long time she just sat by herself in the darkened living room, her thoughts raking over the past she had tried so hard to forget.

Luke Dillon had been her older brother's best friend. The three of them had been inseparable, growing up on Bainbridge Island on adjoining small farms, swimming, hiking, riding bicycles together. It was always taken for granted as they grew older that she and Luke were a pair.

Her brother, Neal, had gone away to college. Luke had to stay home to run the family farm. His father had died years ago, and his mother and older sister depended on him. After Neal was gone, it was just Luke and Katherine. Except when she was in school or he was working, they were constantly together.

She remembered the first time he had ever kissed her. They had been swimming in the Sound and were lying contentedly side by side on the sandy beach. She had sensed him watching her and could feel the tension growing between them. Suddenly Luke had flung himself on top of her and awkwardly covered her mouth with his.

It was the first kiss for both of them. From then on their relationship changed. They found new delight in their embraces and kisses, in exploring each other's bodies, always stopping in time, saving the ultimate act for marriage.

Then, suddenly, when Luke was nineteen, his mother died. A few months later Althea, his older sister, went off to study music in New York, and Luke was free at last to live his own life.

He sold the small farm, divided the proceeds with Althea, and accepted a football scholarship at Stanford. He was finally able to pursue his one ambition, to go to law school. As soon as Katherine graduated from high school they would marry.

She missed him dreadfully. They had been so close all their lives as to be like one person, and she felt as though the other half of herself was missing.

He couldn't afford to come home for a visit and only scrawled an occasional note to her to let her know he was still alive. Reserved and secretive by nature, he was unable to articulate his love for her in a letter, and gradually Katherine began to snap out of her lonely grief and take part in school activities.

She had turned into a beauty by the time she was a senior in high school, and was much sought after, particularly by Brian Croft, son of one of the wealthy families on Bainbridge Island. She hadn't seen Luke for a year and hadn't heard from him for a month when she finally, reluctantly, began dating Brian Croft.

There was no spark, no passion as there had been with Luke, but Brian was smooth, good-looking, had his own car, money to spend and seemed to be crazy about her.

It was one night after a dance when Brian had driven her home that she finally let him kiss her, a tame, soft, tentative kiss. They were at the front door of her house. As he held her in his arms she felt only boredom and found herself staring past him, eyes wide open. She was startled to see a figure standing in the bushes behind the enormous walnut tree in the front of the house.

As the figure came closer she could see that it was Luke. By the light burning on the front porch she recognised him immediately. He gave her one long look and strode towards her. She broke away from Brian and ran to meet Luke, to explain. She was frightened of his reaction, but she was so glad to see him her heart leapt within her.

When she reached him, her arms open wide, his name on her lips, he grabbed her upper arms and held her at a distance. His hold tightened until she cried out in pain. Then he turned and walked off into the darkness.

She never saw him or heard from him again, until yesterday, in Jim Hawkins' office.

Now she felt she had no choice. Earlier, when she had said goodbye to Luke's disdainful good-night, she meant it as a permanent farewell. After what had happened tonight her only alternative seemed to be to quit her job. She could never bear to face Luke Dillon again.

After an hour of painful brooding, Katherine got up from the couch and switched on the lamp. She blinked against the sudden brightness, but with the light came perspective, a sense of reality as opposed to the nightmare she had been living through in her mind.

As she drew the curtains shut she glanced around the cosy room she had decorated with such love and care. The carpet was off-white, the upholstery flowered chintz and deep cherry velveteen. In one corner was her mother's old spinet piano, in another the new stereo set she had bought with her last Christmas bonus.

She switched on the hi-fi. The buoyant refreshing strains of a Brandenburg Concerto filled the room.

She went into the kitchen, put on some coffee and rummaged in the refrigerator, suddenly ravenous after the emotional ordeal. She made a meal of leftover ham and potato salad.

After her supper she took a cup of coffee out into the garden. It was cool outside, but there was a full moon and the stars shone brightly in the black, cloudless sky.

She stood in her rose garden, the scent of the flowers filling the air, and felt the tattered and raw edges of her life begin to weave together again and heal.

As she crawled wearily into bed that night she decided that she couldn't let Luke Dillon drive her out of her job. She knew there were other jobs.

Good, experienced legal secretaries were always in demand. But she liked the job she had. Jim had said the case might settle soon, then Luke would go back to New York and out of her life for good. As she drifted into a troubled sleep, she had made up her mind. She would wait him out.

CHAPTER THREE

THE next day in the coffee room, the burning topic of conversation on everyone's lips was the office party. It seemed that Katherine had missed the best part by leaving so early.

'Not that I blame you,' Irene Connors drawled suggestively. 'You walked off with the prize. How was it?'

'How was what?' Katherine asked calmly as she sipped her coffee.

Irene leaned across the table and leered at her. Katherine noticed the circles under her eyes in spite of the thick make-up, accentuated by the heavy mascara and eye-shadow Irene always wore.

'Oh, come on, Miss Priss, don't play the innocent with me! You were already half undressed when you and Luke Dillon raced out of here.'

Her voice dripped malice, and Katherine groaned inwardly as she suddenly remembered the discarded jacket and scarf, probably still in the rest-room. However, she hadn't patiently and carefully built up her remote, sexless image over the past two years for nothing. This morning, since the sky had clouded over, she had on her most severe outfit, a charcoal brown flannel suit and cream coloured blouse that tied at the neck in a floppy but sedate bow. Her hair was swept back in its usual silken bun.

She sat up a little straighter in her chair, adjusted the bridge of her glasses on her nose and put on her most austere expression.

'Believe it or not, Irene,' she said coolly and firmly, 'Mr Dillon gave me a lift home and that's all.'

Her tone clearly implied that the subject was closed. Irene snorted in disbelief and might have insisted on continuing her probing conversation if Teresa hadn't intervened.

'Say, Irene,' she said sweetly, 'I sure enjoyed that dance you performed on the table last night. I could see that Mr Powell obviously did, too. Poor old guy, you almost gave him a heart attack every time you leaned over in that low-cut dress!'

Irene glared at her and stood up abruptly. 'Bitch,' she muttered under her breath as she stalked off.

Teresa grinned happily at Katherine, who was having trouble suppressing a smile. Then Teresa leaned across the table conspiratorially.

'Come on, honey, give. What did happen?'

'I told you,' Katherine replied lightly, 'absolutely nothing. I decided to go home—you know I don't like that kind of party—and Mr Dillon happened to be going my way. Believe me,' she added as they got up from the table, 'I don't even like him. He's arrogant and conceited.'

They rinsed out their coffee cups at the sink and started down the hall towards their desks.

'Well,' Teresa remarked as she settled down at her typewriter, 'I'd say he's got a lot to be conceited about. Sharon has got to know his secretary in New

York over the telephone, and she says that he's considered *the* catch of the legal profession, that women fall all over themselves to go out with him.'

From her desk, Katherine pushed her glasses down on her nose and peered over them at Teresa. 'His secretary actually *said* such a thing?' she asked incredulously. 'I can hardly believe that.'

'Well,' Teresa muttered, 'she *implied* it.' The typewriter keys started clacking. 'Oh, by the way,' she added, 'I hear through the grapevine that Selma Boyd-Richards got herself assigned to the paper case.'

Katherine gave her a quick look. 'I don't believe it. Selma hates anti-trust. After that last fiasco when Judge Meehan yelled at her she said she'd never go near federal court again.'

'That was before she got a load of Luke Dillon,' said Teresa.

'Oh, come on, Teresa—Selma's married!'

Teresa snorted. 'Sure, to Mr Richards. They have what is known as an open marriage—you know, you do your thing, I'll do mine.'

'Why even bother being married?' Katherine asked.

'Beats me,' Teresa replied. 'I'd like to catch Tony pulling a stunt like that on me!' Her dark eyes flashed fire.

Selma Boyd-Richards was not Katherine's favourite lawyer. She demanded all the prerogatives of a man, yet had no compunction about using her femininity to get what she wanted. Katherine sighed. If it were true, this new development would only add to the ordeal ahead.

Katherine reached for the papers in the wooden tray, and her eyes fastened on the glass paperweight. She picked it up and put it at the back of her bottom drawer. Just the sight of it brought back painful memories of the night before that she was determined to forget. Luke had given it to her for her sixteenth birthday and she'd had it close by her ever since, even during her short disastrous marriage to Brian Croft.

Funny, she thought, as she began sorting the documents into neat piles, she never really thought of those few weeks as a marriage. She hadn't been in love with Brian, but he was attractive and could offer her security when she had lost Luke so suddenly and brutally. After he'd stalked off that night she tried to get in touch with him, to explain, but he returned all her letters unopened and didn't have a telephone.

She had considered once getting on a plane and going down there to find him, but by then her pride was so wounded by his totally irrational behaviour that it was less painful to live without him than continue to pursue him when he obviously didn't want her.

By then he had made a name for himself as a star quarterback on the Stanford football team, and Katherine began to believe that he probably had other girls by now who were more exciting than his friend's little sister.

Then there was Brian, so ardent before their wedding, so cold after. Katherine hadn't loved him the way she had Luke, but she was a normal girl with normal instincts, and she wanted children.

When she finally realised that the reason her husband never came near her, never even touched her when they were alone, was because his sexual preferences lay elsewhere, that he had only married her as a front for his sick tendencies, she became convinced that love and marriage were not in the cards for her.

First Luke, she thought, then Brian. Two men she had cared for, and both rejected her.

'Well, Miss Croft, are we going to get some work done today, or are you going to sit mooning into space all morning?'

Luke's voice cut into her thoughts like a cracking whip. She glanced up at him. He stood at her desk looking down at her, eyes narrowed, mouth in a cruel sardonic line.

Very well, she thought to herself as she recovered her composure, if that's the way you're going to play it, I'll join you.

'Just what was it you needed, Mr Dillon?' she asked icily, her hazel eyes hard.

'I don't like your filing system,' he said curtly.

'The firm has a standard system it uses throughout the office,' she said evenly. 'I didn't invent it. I only follow orders.'

'Good,' he said. 'I have a few for you. Come into my office.'

He stalked off. Katherine took her time finding her notebook, stopped to sharpen a pencil and considered seriously walking out of the office, the building and Luke Dillon's life completely. She saw Teresa staring at her, wide-eyed. Katherine grinned at the expression on her face and shrugged.

'See what I mean?' she said clearly. 'Arrogant, conceited and a bully, to boot.'

Teresa was horrified. 'Shh!' she hissed. 'He'll hear you!'

'So?' Katherine replied. Slowly, with dignity, she made her way into Luke's office.

He sat at the desk glaring at her.

'Shut the door,' he barked.

'Yes, sir,' she said sweetly, and took her time doing so.

When she turned back to him, every movement slow and deliberate, he was leaning back in the swivel chair, arms folded in front of him, gazing up at her fiercely from under a thunderous brow.

'Don't hurry on my account,' he said nastily. 'There's only a million-dollar law suit at stake.'

He had on a navy blue suit with the faintest of pin stripes. The colour made his hair seem blue-black in the light from the window. Katherine noticed with a slight shock the creases at the corners of his eyes. He isn't even thirty, she thought, and yet he looks so mature and, yes, tired. Quickly she banished any such sentimental considerations from her mind. This man is my enemy, she reminded herself.

He stood up and in two quick strides crossed over to the filing cabinet against the window wall.

'If you'll be so kind as to step over here, Miss Croft—or should it be Mrs Croft?' he asked, turning to look her up and down.

'It's Miss,' she said flatly. 'No one here knows I was married, and I'd appreciate it if you didn't mention it.'

'Just like that,' he commented. He propped himself against the filing cabinet and snapped his fingers. 'Goodbye, marriage, as if it never happened. You really have a knack for getting rid of men you have no more use for!'

'You mentioned some filing,' she said coldly.

She was having trouble controlling her temper under his needling. She knew that if she ever let him arouse any emotion in her whatsoever, she'd be lost. As she watched him, his arrogant posture, the elegant cut of his beautifully tailored suit, the crisp white shirt, the strong domineering chin and lithe figure, her mind threatened to spill over into chaos. She hated him more than she had ever thought it possible to hate anyone, yet his presence in the room jolted her against her will into an intense awareness of his sheer animal magnetism.

'Ah, yes,' he said, 'the filing. As I say, I don't like your system.'

'It's not *my* system,' she began.

He raised a hand. 'I don't care whose system it is. I'm running this case, and we'll file these documents my way.'

She sighed. 'It will mean redoing the whole thing, four full drawers of documents.'

'Then we'd better start,' he said with satisfaction. 'Get some help, work overtime, but just get it done.'

There was a sharp rap on the door and a tall woman with flaming red hair strode into the room. Ignoring Katherine entirely, she crossed immediately over to Luke. She stood with her hands squarely set on well-proportioned hips. Katherine noticed that the long, well-curved body was displayed enticingly in a clinging purple wool jersey dress.

'*Bonjour*, Luke,' came a throaty purr. 'I see you're hard at it already.' She moved a step closer to him. 'I thought I'd just toddle along this morning to get filled in on the case.'

She reached up gleaming purple fingernails to pick off a piece of lint from Luke's lapel. A lazy grin appeared on his face as he looked down at the tempting redhead, and their eyes met in a sudden, tacit understanding.

Oh, no, Katherine thought. I don't have to stand here and watch the great seduction scene, although it wasn't quite clear who was seducing whom. She turned and marched determinedly to the door. When her hand was on the knob, Luke's voice rang out.

'Wait a minute,' he snapped. 'I didn't say we were finished.'

She looked at him over her shoulder. 'That's right,' she said, giving her sweetest smile, 'you didn't.'

She opened the door and walked out of the room. With a great deal of satisfaction she heard Selma Boyd-Richards' incredulous gasp.

She crossed over to her desk, knees suddenly weak. Her telephone was ringing. With trembling fingers she picked it up and answered it.

'This is Katherine Croft,' she said, fighting to keep the tremor out of her voice.

'Hi, honey, it's me,' came a warm familiar voice.

'Oh, Jim,' she breathed, 'I'm so glad to hear your voice!'

'Hey, I'll have to go out of town more often if that's what my absence does to you!'

'You're like a breath of fresh air after Mr Dillon and Ms Boyd-Richards,' she said bitterly.

He paused. 'Like that, huh?'

'Like that,' she said.

'I'm sorry, Katherine. I'll do what I can for you, but my hands are pretty well tied. It won't be for ever.'

'Listen,' she said quickly, 'don't worry about it. I'm tougher than I look. Any hope of settlement— soon?'

'Afraid not. That's why I called. The guy I'm deposing got suspiciously sick all of a sudden just as it looked as though I was getting somewhere with him.'

'Oh, I'm sorry, Jim.'

'Anyway, there is a bright spot. I'm coming back to Seattle tonight. Thought maybe you could get my car and pick me up at the airport. My plane gets in at five-thirty, so you'll have to leave work early. Okay?'

'More than okay,' she breathed.

'What's the weather like?'

She glanced out the window. 'Cloudy, but it looks like it might be clearing.'

'Let's go out to dinner at that new place on Shilshole Bay. Why don't you make the reservations?'

When she hung up the phone she felt like a new woman. Bless Jim Hawkins! she said to herself.

That afternoon Katherine decided she'd better leave the office at two-thirty if she hoped to go to the garage where Jim kept his car when he was out of town, go home and change and get to the airport by five-thirty.

She told Teresa where she was going, grabbed her jacket and started past Luke Dillon's office just as he opened his door. He was in his shirtsleeves.

'Where do you think you're going?' he asked belligerently, hands on his hips.

He towered over her, glaring, but the comfort and support she had derived from her phone conversation with Jim Hawkins fortified her against his onslaught. She stood before him, looking up at him, her head cocked to one side. She smiled wickedly.

'Wherever I happen to feel like going,' she announced, and turned to walk off.

A powerful hand clamped itself on her arm and she felt herself being pulled bodily into his office. Luke shut the door, backed her against the wall and spread out his arms, his hands flattened on the wall at either side of her head.

He was so close she could feel his harsh breathing, see the little pulse pounding in his jaw as he glared at her. Their bodies were not quite touching, but the tiny space between them was charged like a magnet.

'Now listen to me,' he muttered through clenched teeth. 'I've about had it with that smart mouth of yours!'

Katherine rolled her eyes and pulled her shoulders back defiantly, not realising how provocative the gesture was. With the movement, the tips of her full breasts, straining against the silky material of her blouse, just barely touched the front of his shirt.

'Oh, my,' she mocked, 'you do terrify me, Mr Dillon!'

She saw the sudden fire flash in his dark eyes, and for a brief moment she thought he was going to hit her. She didn't even care. After the humiliating pain he had inflicted on her last night, nothing he could do now could possibly be worse.

Instead, he bent down swiftly and clamped his mouth on hers, pushing his long lean body against her, his strong hard thighs pinning her to the wall.

She tried to move her head, but he was too strong for her, the pressure of his mouth on hers too overwhelming. She tried to bite him, but this merely made it easier for him to force her mouth open for his penetrating invasion of it.

Still she struggled. She raised her fists and beat on his arms. He was like a rock. Then she felt a hand move between them and grasp her breast, kneading it roughly, then stroking it more gently. It's not fair, she moaned to herself, as the hand slid under her blouse to tease the hardening nipple underneath. His touch sent a piercing shaft of desire through her whole body.

As she began to melt against him, he released her mouth and buried his head in her hair, loosened from the struggle and streaming around her face.

'God, Katie,' he breathed in her ear, 'you're so beautiful!'

Katherine felt as though she were drowning, as

though she and Luke were back once again on the island, alone in their private world. The familiar contours of the body pressed against her, the taste of the hot mouth so recently welded with her own, the feel of the crisp dark hair on her face.

No, a voice screamed inside her head. No! Summoning all her strength, she slipped out of the vice of his rough embrace and stood to one side, panting, straightening her clothes, smoothing her hair.

He was still leaning up against the wall, his forehead pressed against it, his arms over his head, his shoulders heaving. Katherine reached out a hand towards him, then quickly drew it back, knowing she would be lost if she touched him again. She finished pinning her hair up and hurried to the door.

'If you ever lay a hand on me again, Luke Dillon,' she said evenly, 'I'll walk out of this office and never come back. But not before I've told everyone here why.'

Slowly, he turned around to face her. His face was a mask. He stared at her for a full minute, then said, 'All right, I guess I asked for that. God knows I don't want to get burned in your flame again. Once is enough to last a man a lifetime.'

'Have it your way, Luke,' she said wearily. 'I've done all the explaining I'm going to do about the past. You're so full of self-pity and wounded male ego that you won't listen anyway. But since we're going to have to work together on this case, let's just try a little common courtesy.'

'Do you suppose we could begin that regime,' he asked, totally in possession of himself again, 'by your telling me where you're going? That's all I asked, you know. You provoked me. When I'm working on a case it's all I have on my mind. I need you this afternoon.'

'That's fair enough,' she admitted. She lowered her eyes, ashamed now of her childish sarcasm. 'I'm going to pick Jim up at the airport.'

His mind was immediately on the case. 'What happened to the deposition?'

'The deponent got sick. They had to call it off.'

'Oh, hell,' Luke muttered. 'There are a dozen ways around that old ploy. We needed that deposition—now. He's a key witness. Didn't Jim even try?'

'I'm sure he did,' said Katherine rising to Jim's defence. 'He'll be in the office tomorrow. You can discuss it then.'

'I guess that'll have to do,' he said. He sat down at his desk and turned his full attention to his work. Katherine slipped quietly out of the door.

A pale sun did finally break through the canopy of clouds late in the afternoon. Jim and Katherine took a table by the window overlooking the Sound. The restaurant sat at the end of a long pier, just north of the locks that lowered boats from the inland fresh water into the salt water of Puget Sound.

They watched the intermittent clusters of boats sailing out of the locks on their way across the Sound, and an occasional flash of silver betokened a salmon leaping in the air.

They had ordered dinner, King salmon barbecued Indian style over an alder fire, and sat sipping their drinks. Jim had ordered a Martini, Katherine a glass of cream sherry.

Jim had been watching her carefully ever since they had sat down across from each other. Now he leaned back in the seat, one hand tipping his cocktail back and forth idly.

'You look different, Katherine,' he said slowly, his eyes fastened on her face.

She looked up quickly. 'Different?' She smiled. 'How, different?'

He leaned forward, elbows on the table, his brow knitted in a puzzled frown. 'I don't know. It's hard to explain. You know I've always been highly—and very vocally—appreciative of your beauty, but tonight you seem—I don't know—somehow rather ruffled. You're always so cool, so remote, so—well,' he laughed, 'almost virginally aloof. Now, you seem warmer. Oh, hell,' he laughed again, 'I'm saying this badly. I mean it as a compliment, but it doesn't seem to be coming out that way.'

He reached across the table and took her hand in his. Instinctively she started to draw it back. Then she noticed the hurt look on his face and decided it could do no harm, implied no commitment, to allow him to hold her hand, for heaven's sake.

'Why do you always fight me?' he asked, his eyes pleading.

She leaned towards him. 'I don't mean to fight you, Jim,' she said softly. 'I just don't want to lead you to expect more from me than I can deliver.'

'Have I ever pushed?' he asked. 'Forced any issues?'

She lowered her eyes and shook her head slowly. 'No, Jim, you've always been a perfect gentleman. And I appreciate it.' Not like some people, she thought bitterly.

Gradually Katherine began to relax. Jim was so easy to be with, she thought, so comforting. The sun was going down now below the crest of the Olympic Mountains to the west, casting a reddish glow in the still blue sky. The water was calm, with only an occasional gentle ripple or darting salmon breaking its unruffled stillness.

Soft music played in the background. From the other tables came the low hum of muted conversations, an occasional burst of laughter, the pleasant clinking of silverware and china.

She glanced happily around the room and found herself staring directly into the smouldering dark eyes of Luke Dillon. By his side, hanging on to his arm, was Selma Boyd-Richards. Hastily she withdrew her hand from Jim's and looked away.

'Oh, no!' she groaned.

'What's wrong?' Jim asked. 'Don't you feel well?'

'Look who's here,' she said disgustedly.

Jim turned in his seat. Selma caught his eye and began to thread her way through the crowded room, skirting the tables, her hips moving sensuously—for Luke's benefit, of course, Katherine thought. She wondered just how an open marriage worked. She assumed it was one which gave total freedom to the other party.

Katherine believed firmly that she would probably never marry. She had been in love, wildly and passionately, with all the strength of her being, just once in her life, with Luke Dillon. After that heady experience she knew nothing less would ever satisfy her. But if she ever did marry, she thought now, it would never be the kind of open marriage Selma seemed to enjoy. She could never share her man with other women. She would want a real home, children.

She glanced across the table at Jim, at the expression on his face as he watched Selma undulating slowly towards them to get the maximum effect out of the swaying of her long, well-curved figure. Katherine saw that there was no trace of desire on his face, only a kind of tolerant amusement.

I could have a good life with Jim, she thought, if that's what I really wanted. Except, she added, that I don't love him. And life alone was better than life in a loveless marriage.

Selma was at their table now. Luke seemed to have disappeared. From the glazed look in the redhead's eyes, Katherine concluded that she had already had a few drinks.

Selma put the heels of her hands firmly on the table, upsetting a glass of water as she did so. The top buttons of her bright purple dress were undone, and as she leaned over it was immediately obvious that the rumours about her were quite true. She was indeed bra-less.

Katherine started mopping up the spilled water. She glanced covertly at Jim, wide-eyed by now, his gaze fastened on Selma's almost completely exposed bosom.

'Well, look who's here,' Selma drawled. She turned around, her eyes searching the room. 'Mind if we join you? I don't know what happened to Luke.'

She slid on to the upholstered bench next to Jim. Katherine groaned inwardly. She felt trapped. There was no way to leave gracefully; their dinner hadn't even been served yet. She would have to stay where she was. Might as well just grit my teeth and make the best of it, she thought. If I'm going to work with him I'll have to get used to being around him.'

'What happened in San Francisco, Jim?' Selma asked. 'I thought you weren't due back until Friday.'

Jim began to explain the sudden illness of the witness. Selma listened intently, stopping only to order a drink. It was as though Katherine didn't exist—not when there was a man around. Katherine didn't care; she was content to gaze out at the water and watch the boats go by.

Then she felt a presence at her side. She flinched a little, turned, and saw that Luke was sitting beside her. She began to feel uncomfortably warm, even though the sun had set. Selma and Jim were discussing the case, deep in conversation. As Katherine watched them, she got the distinct impression that Selma was performing for Luke's benefit. Her laugh was a little forced, her voice a shade too loud, her gestures overdone.

Although she wouldn't have glanced his way for worlds, Katherine was intensely aware of the silent man beside her. He was sitting perfectly still. Her cheeks burned with the memory of their angry exchange earlier today in the office.

Suddenly, over the drone of the music and the conversation across the table, she heard Luke's voice speaking to her in a low tone. She jumped a little and turned to face him.

'Sorry,' she said, 'I didn't hear you.'

'I asked you if you'd care to dance.'

She was so surprised she could only stare at him. He stood up and beckoned to her.

'Come on,' he ordered.

Numbly she obeyed and started to slide across the bench. She glanced at Jim, but he was deep in an explanation of something to Selma about the case.

As they walked on to the tiny dance floor, Katherine wondered what game Luke was playing now. He took her hand lightly in his and put an arm around her waist. They began to dance.

His touch was impersonal. He held her loosely, their bodies barely touching.

'How is Neal?' he asked finally.

'Quite well,' she answered, her voice stiff.

'Still here in Seattle?'

'Yes.'

'Married?'

'Yes.'

He gave her a little shake and looked down at her with irritation.

'Relax, Katherine, for God's sake! I'm not going to create a scene.'

She stiffened. 'Every word you've spoken to me since you came to the office has either been an accusation or an order,' she muttered.

She glanced surreptitiously up at him through a thick curtain of eyelashes and surprised a self-satisfied grin on his lean face. In reply he tightened his grip on her and pulled her a little closer.

'I thought we called a truce,' he said lightly.

He was right. She had to agree. If they were going to work together they'd have to try to get along. It was unfortunate that they had to bump into each other socially tonight, and she intended to try to avoid such occasions in the future.

'You're right,' she said, giving him a cool smile. 'Now, I think our dinner has arrived. We'd better get back to the table.'

Gradually Katherine's self-possession began to return. Luke had shaken her badly, but now it appeared he had come to terms with the past at last. She felt relieved, even glad it had happened. Yet, walking ahead of him back to the table, his hand lightly under her elbow, guiding her through the crowd, she could hardly suppress a momentary pang of regret.

CHAPTER FOUR

As the weeks passed into July, the weather became warmer and the paper case progressed at the usual snail-like pace. Jim Hawkins was gone from the office at depositions and document inspection more than he was there.

Luke had been spending most of his time preparing for one of the few interesting events in the early stages of an anti-trust case. The defendants on the other side had filed a motion for summary judgement, in effect asking the judge to dismiss the case on the basis that the plaintiff didn't have sufficient legal grounds for a case. It was standard procedure, a routine move in the game of law, but still it required an argument before the judge and the preparation of a reply to the motion. At least it generated a little excitement and required intensive preparation.

With Jim gone from the office so much, Katherine had virtually become Luke's private secretary. He conducted all the correspondence and settlement negotiations with the other side and made all the decisions pertinent to the lawsuit. Katherine knew that he and Selma spent long hours together in the evening and at weekends supposedly working on the case. She couldn't help wondering occasionally just how far their personal relationship had progressed. She tried to banish such thoughts from her mind as soon as they arose.

One Friday morning Luke called Katherine into his office as soon as she arrived at her desk. She picked up a notebook and pencil and went inside. He was sitting at his desk, a document in his hands.

'Sit down,' he said without looking up at her.

She sat across from him waiting for his instructions. The air-conditioning was on, but Luke's office was on the east side of the building and the sun shone brightly through the window, warming the room.

Katherine had worn her light blue linen skirt with the paler blue cotton knit shell and a while linen jacket. She was getting warmer by the minute. The sun shone directly on her. She set down her pad and pencil on the desk and stretched her arms back to take off her jacket.

'Don't do that!' she heard Luke snap.

She glanced at him in surprise. 'Don't do what?' she asked blankly. 'It's hot in here.'

Then she saw that his dark smouldering eyes were riveted to the front of her shell. She flushed and slipped the jacket over her shoulders so it draped loosely in front of her.

Luke's eyes moved to meet hers. 'I don't know how I'm supposed to concentrate on my work when you flaunt yourself like that,' he said irritably.

Katherine opened her mouth to protest hotly. Then she realised he was baiting her.

'Sorry,' she murmured coolly. 'I forgot for a moment you were here.'

He glared at her. She gave him a demure look

and smoothed her hair. He went back to his document.

'Okay,' he said finally. 'This will be a pleading in the paper case. Title, 'Plaintiff's Reply to Defendants' Motion for Summary Judgement.' ' He got up and started pacing around the room.

Katherine took the title down in shorthand, then looked up at him in surprise. 'Excuse me,' she said. 'When is the hearing on this motion?'

He paused in his pacing and raised an eyebrow at her. 'August the third. Why?'

Her eyes widened. 'That's three weeks away.'

He placed the knuckles of his hands on the desk and leaned toward her. 'So?' he asked. 'What's so significant about that?'

She stammered out a reply. 'Well, it's just that I've never known a lawyer who didn't wait until the last minute to work on a reply to a motion.'

'I don't operate that way,' Luke said flatly. 'Now, if it's all right with you, may we proceed?'

He started pacing again, silent for a full minute while he collected his thoughts. Then he began dictating.

Katherine's pencil raced to keep up with him. His thoughts were so clear, his argument so well thought out, his style of dictating so smooth, that it began to seem as though they were one person, that as soon as the words were out of his mouth, she had them down in her notebook.

He dictated for two hours straight. There were none of the long moments of boredom while the lawyer tried to marshal his ideas. No hemming and hawing. No curt command to strike out a phrase six

pages back or insert one at the beginning. No
telephone interruptions. At the first ring he had
picked up the receiver, barked that he was taking
no calls, and slammed it down again. Then, after
she had read back the previous sentence, he went
right on with that easy, concise flow of words.

When he finally finished, Katherine was exhausted, her fingers numb. She was also deeply
impressed. She doubted if a word would have to be
changed. Never had she encountered such clarity of
thought or such cogency of expression. He knew
exactly what he wanted to say, and he said it
without hesitation.

'Okay,' he said at last, 'that's it for now. Type it
up and let me have it in draft. Make two copies.'

She leaned back in the chair, worn out, and
looked at him. The jacket had long since slipped
unnoticed from her shoulders in her urgency to
keep up with him.

'I . . .' she began, then stumbled. How do you
compliment such a man? she wondered.

Luke darted a look at her. 'Well? What is it?' His
eyes widened. 'Dear God,' he breathed, horrified,
'don't tell me you didn't get it all down!'

'Oh, I got it all down,' she hastened to reassure
him. 'It's just that—well, I'm impressed.' Her mouth
twisted into a grudging smile.

His heavy dark eyebrows shot up. 'Oh, really?'
he drawled sarcastically.

'Yes, really,' she snapped. She got to her feet
thinking she should have known better than to try
to say something nice to him.

She picked up the jacket and slipped it over her

shoulders again, fully aware that he was watching her every movement. Their eyes met briefly, his dark and brooding, hers flashing with irritation. A brief current passed between them. Then he smiled sardonically, looked her up and down insolently and dropped his eyes to the papers on his desk.

She turned on her heel and marched out the door. Teresa was at Katherine's desk waiting for her when she emerged.

'Wow,' she whispered, 'that was quite a session! You can't tell me it was all work and no play.'

'Oh, no?' Katherine said wearily. She shuffled her notebook at her to show her the pages of shorthand. 'Take a look at that.'

Teresa's eyes widened. 'Did you get it all down?'

Katherine rolled her eyes heavenward. 'Lord help me if I didn't!'

Teresa's glance suddenly flicked past her. 'Don't look now,' she hissed, 'but I think it's half-time.' Katherine looked a question at her. 'Boyd-Richards,' Teresa said. 'In the clinging white knit. Just went into Dillon's lair.'

Katherine shrugged. 'They deserve each other.'

She sat down at her desk and started typing. She could re-read her own notes easily, she noticed thankfully after she had set up the complex heading. Under the local rules for federal court the name, address and telephone number of each attorney involved in the case had to be typed in on the title page, followed by the name of the party they represented. In this case there were twelve attorneys.

'Lunchtime,' Teresa announced. 'Did you bring

a sandwich? It's a gorgeous day. Let's walk up to the Freeway Park, there's going to be a bluegrass band concert today.'

Katherine frowned. 'Oh, Teresa, I don't think so. I'll just get a Coke and eat my sandwich at my desk. I want to get out of here by five tonight so I can catch the commuter ferry.'

'Another sizzling weekend at your brother's?' Teresa asked.

'Mm-hmm,' Katherine murmured absently. She gestured towards the small overnight case behind her desk against the wall.

'My, how thrilling,' Teresa commented drily. 'I can think of better things to do with my weekend.'

Katherine looked up at her with a quick grin. 'I'm sure you can, Teresa. How are things with you and Tony?'

Teresa shrugged and rolled her eyes. 'Oh, you know—just about the same. Fight like cats and dogs all day, make love all night.' She sighed. 'I just can't seem to live without him, the rat. Well, don't work too hard,' she called back over her shoulder as she went off down the hall.

Under her breath Katherine uttered a short prayer of thanksgiving that she was not bound body and soul to a man who mistreated her the way Tony did Teresa. He either drank or gambled their money away, had trouble holding down a job, and while Katherine didn't believe he had ever actually been unfaithful to the fiery little Italian girl, he did have a roving eye.

Yet, she thought, as she started typing, she had

half envied them whenever she'd seen them together. Every time they touched, sparks seemed to leap between them. No, she thought firmly, it's not worth it.

At one o'clock, just as Katherine was finishing her sandwich at her desk, she saw Sharon, the receptionist, go up to Luke's door with a white sack from the delicatessen downstairs. She rapped tentatively at the door, looking over at Katherine meaningfully, rolling her eyes and grinning. Luke and Selma, Katherine thought, as she gave Sharon a little wave, were having lunch together in his office. Or something.

She typed straight through her afternoon coffee break and by five o'clock she was so stiff from sitting in one position all day, her fingers so sore, her eyes so crossed, that she decided to quit, even though she had about five more pages of notes to go.

As usual on a sunny Friday afternoon, the office had been completely deserted by four-thirty, and Katherine was alone. She picked up the stack of typed pages and took them into Luke's office. Selma had gone, but he was still there. He was standing at the window, fully engrossed in the law book he held in his hands.

Katherine put the pages down on his desk. 'I'll just leave these here,' she announced. 'I didn't quite finish, but I think there's enough for you to work on over the weekend. There are only a few more pages to go.

He put his finger on his place in the book and gave her a dark look.

'I need the whole thing,' he announced flatly. 'Surely you can stay long enough to finish a few pages?'

She tried to keep her voice even. 'I really can't. I have a ferry to catch.'

He raised heavy dark eyebrows. 'Isn't there a later ferry?'

'Yes, but I'm being met on the other side.'

'Call him and tell him you're taking a later ferry,' he said. He went back to his reading.

Anger began to boil up in Katherine. She never minded working overtime as a rule, but Jim rarely asked her to do so, and then only with profuse apologies. This male chauvinist pig just took it for granted she'd drop all her plans for him.

'Listen,' she said, making an effort to control herself, 'I've been typing all day, and I've had it. There's enough there for you to work on.'

Luke glared at her. 'I need the whole thing,' he said, one word coming precisely after another, like bullets from a gun.

She glared back, no longer attempting to control her fury. 'Well, that's too bad, because I'm leaving.' She marched to the door, paused and turned her head. 'Maybe you can get Ms Boyd-Richards to type it for you—if she can type!'

Her cheeks were burning. She went to her desk to get her overnight case, wondering what in the world had made her say such a childish thing. She grabbed the bag and hurried past Luke's office towards the elevator.

Luke was at the door watching her. His eyes moved to the overnight case and lingered there for a moment. Then he gave her a look that bespoke deep contempt.

'Ah, now I see why you were in such a hurry,' he drawled maddeningly. 'It's to be one of those weekends.'

'Think what you like,' she muttered, and rushed past him.

'Damn you!' he roared, and grabbed her by the arm so that he took her off balance and she started to fall.

He gripped her arm firmly, steadying her, then grabbed her other arm and held her so that she couldn't move.

'You're the most insufferable, insubordinate secretary it has even been my misfortune to work with!' he growled at her between clenched teeth.

'You're hurting me!' she cried out. 'You always were a bully, and you haven't changed a bit!' To her horror she felt tears sting her eyes. 'Now you've made me miss my ferry!' she heard herself blubber like a child. She'd like to kill him for reducing her to this.

'Oh, stop it!' he barked, releasing her arms abruptly. 'And you always were a crybaby.'

'I was not,' she sniffled, rummaging in her bag for a handkerchief. She wiped her eyes, blew her nose and glared at him.

He was facing her, hands on his hips, a strange expression on his face that Katherine couldn't quite fathom. He appeared angry still, but something in his eyes showed a hint of concern.

'You were always in tears,' he insisted. 'Every time you'd fall down or get stung by a little bee or we'd run off and leave you, you'd dissolve in tears.'

'Sure,' she said heatedly, 'when I broke my arm, when I was stung by a whole nest full of bees, when you and Neal hid from me for a whole day. You knew I wanted to go hiking with you.'

Suddenly, as if at some hidden, automatic signal, they both started to laugh as the storehouse of memories they shared from earliest childhood came bubbling to the surface.

'Well, this looks cosy,' came a female voice. 'What's so hilarious?'

Katherine wheeled around. Selma Boyd-Richards was at the door, bra-less in her clinging white knit dress that left nothing whatsoever to the imagination. There was a smile on her face, but she did not look amused.

Katherine sobered down instantly. 'Mr Dillon will explain, Selma,' she said sweetly. 'I've got to run to catch the next ferry.' On an impulse she turned back to Luke. 'He'll be furious if I'm late!' Then she left.

Katherine did just barely make the next ferry. Luckily a bus came right along that went to the Ferry Terminal at the foot of Marion Street. The last foot passengers were just straggling on as she jumped off the bus and ran up the ramp to join them.

The ferry hooted, bells rang, chains clanked, and they began slowly to chug out of the harbour. The sides of the boat squeaked against the tall wooden pilings along the dock.

Katherine went up to the top deck and leaned

over the railing. The salt air was tangy in her nose
and mouth, and she breathed it in deeply. There
was a soft breeze. She turned into it, letting it caress
her face and pull a few strands loose from her
securely pinned honey gold hair. The water was a
glassy blue, the western sun cutting a wide golden
swath through it just ahead of them. Seagulls
screeched, wheeling and dipping in the cloudless
sky.

It was a short trip to Bainbridge Island, less than
half an hour. As Katherine stepped off the ferry on
the other side, she spotted her brother Neal leaning
against the wooden railing at the top of the harbour. When he saw her walking up the ramp he
straightened up, glanced meaningfully at his watch
and shot her a black look.

Katherine sighed. Neal was a rising young aero-
nautical engineer in charge of a whole design sec-
tion at the Boeing Company, Seattle's largest in-
dustry. His time was valuable and organised to the
minute. He did not suffer tardiness gladly.

'Sorry I'm late, Neal,' she began explaining as
soon as possible. 'Last-minute flap at the office.'

He grabbed her suitcase and started off towards
the car. She followed him meekly. Brother and
sister were a great deal alike in appearance, with
the same golden hair and flecked hazel eyes, but
their personalities were direct opposites.

They drove in silence for a while. Neal drove as
he did everything else, with total concentration,
aggression and a kind of hyperactive vitality. He
was a human dynamo. Katherine often worried
that his three packs of unfiltered cigarettes a day,

quarts of coffee, four to five hours' sleep a night and constant movement would kill him off by the time he was forty.

'How are Barbara and Nancy?' Katherine asked as they sped along the narrow road that led to their old family home.

Neal grunted something that sounded affirmative. Katherine, accustomed to his ways and unperturbed by them, watched the scenery fly by out of the car window.

When their parents had been killed in an automobile accident four years ago, Neal had paid Katherine her share of the market value of their home and gone to live there with his wife and daughter. With her share, Katherine had bought her tiny cottage on Queen Anne Hill. Over the past few years Neal and Barbara had completely restored and modernised the old rambling farmhouse and turned the five acres that sloped down to a private beach into a lovely wild garden.

Neal slowed up when they came to the winding road that led down through the towering firs, pines and cedars to the house. It was pleasantly cool in the shade of the giant trees. Neal lit a cigarette.

Katherine turned to him. 'Neal, you'll never guess who showed up at the office about a month ago.' She had debated telling Neal about Luke, not wanting to get anything personal started between them. Now she decided that Neal would probably find out anyway and wonder why she hadn't told him.

'Let me guess,' he said, as he pulled up in front of the house. 'Luke Dillon.'

He turned to her with a wicked grin. Katherine stared at him, open-mouthed.

'How did you know?' she asked, glad now she had told him first thing.

'He called me at the office a few weeks ago. We had lunch.'

He got out of the car, grabbed her suitcase and started to stride down the stepping stones that led to the house. Katherine scrambled out of the car and hurried after him.

'Neal!' she called.

He turned around. 'Come on,' he said irritably. 'You're already late. Barbara wants to eat outside'.

'Neal!' she insisted. He came back a few steps, and she put a hand on his arm.

His face softened. He covered her hand with his own. 'It's okay, Katie,' he said kindly. 'We didn't discuss you at all—that's a closed book. Don't look back.'

Katherine opened her mouth to explain that Luke's sudden appearance in her life had opened that book again with a vegeance, then she changed her mind. Neal would never understand. Besides, his darting mind had already leaped ahead to something else, and as they went into the house he was telling her about his business trip to Africa and the camera safari he had been on.

While Neal went upstairs to put her bag in her old room, now a guest room, Katherine went to the kitchen, at the back of the house, overlooking Puget Sound. Barbara was at the kitchen counter tossing a salad. She was a small woman, with a slim boyish figure and a mop of dark curls cut quite short. She had on shorts and a brief halter and wore sandals on her tiny feet.

'Hi, Katie,' she called out. 'Come and taste this salad and tell me what you think of the dressing. It's a new recipe and I'm not convinced it's going to work.'

Katherine fished out a piece of lettuce, chewed and swallowed. 'Not quite enough anchovy for my taste,' she said thoughtfully, knowing Barbara expected a constructive criticism.

'Oh, good,' Barbara beamed, relieved. 'I knew there was something wrong. Take off that jacket, for heaven's sake. Don't you want to change? You have ten minutes.'

Katherine took off her jacket and while Barbara doctored the salad, she wandered around the familiar old kitchen.

It was a huge room, really a combination family room, dining room and kitchen. It led out on to a wide wooden deck. There was an enormous stone fireplace along one wall, with a braided rug in front of it that Katherine's mother had made.

'I envy you living over here,' Katherine said with a sigh.

Barbara turned around quickly, her face clouding over, 'Oh, Katie, you know you're welcome to come back here to live any time you want.'

At that moment six-year-old Nancy appeared through the sliding glass doors to the deck. She gave Katherine a quick, shy smile and went to her mother's side. She tugged at her shorts and looked up at her.

'Yes, darling,' Barbara murmured absently, still tossing salad.

'Is Aunt Katie coming to live with us?' she whispered.

Katherine turned her head so the little girl wouldn't see the smile on her face. Nancy was as prickly and proud and reserved as she herself had been as a child. She even looks like me, she thought, a sturdy little girl with two thick plaits of honey-coloured hair and scabbed-over knees. She had on denim shorts and a white sleeveless blouse.

'You'll have to ask her,' said Barbara.

Nancy turned shy, questioning eyes on her aunt. Her eyes were hazel, flecked with gold, just like Katherine's and Neal's. Katherine went over to her, stooped down and put a hand lightly on the girl's cheek.

'Afraid not, sweetie. My job is in Seattle.'

'Daddy goes to work in Seattle,' Nancy said reasonably. 'He goes on the ferry.'

Katherine stood up, smoothing her blue linen skirt. 'Your daddy is a much hardier soul than I am,' she said with a little laugh. 'He always was. When I was your age, and he was ten, I was forever trying to keep up with him and Luke.'

Barbara turned and gave her a quick look. Katherine flushed deeply and lowered her eyes. She could have bitten her tongue out. Damn Luke Dillon! Why did he have to come back?

Barbara started to get cutlery out of a drawer. 'Neal told me Luke called him.' she said casually over her shoulder. 'Wasn't that a coincidence, his turning up at your office?'

'Quite a coincidence,' Katherine agreed wryly. She took the cutlery from Barbara's hands. 'Come on, Nancy,' she said, 'let's go set the table.'

After dinner Katherine helped Barbara in the kitchen while Neal and Nancy went for a walk on the beach. The little girl wasn't allowed to go down there alone, and Neal took her every evening. He could never just sit still and talk, as Katherine and Barbara could, but had to be constantly on the move.

'There,' said Barbara when the last dish had been put away in the dishwasher. 'Let's take our coffee out on the deck.'

The two women sat in companionable silence for some time. It was still light out at eight o'clock, but the sun had set and dusk would fall quickly. It was utterly quiet and peaceful, except for the distant toot of an occasional ferry or the screeching of gulls.

Katherine leaned back in the chaise-longue, utterly relaxed, and sipped her coffee. Every time she came over to the island for a visit it brought back a flood of childhood memories. Now, with Luke Dillon's sudden appearance in her life, memory sharpened and became more poignant.

The Dillons had lived on the neighbouring property, eking out a precarious living raising poultry, selling eggs. Mrs Dillon made extra money mending and doing alterations. Luke's older sister, Althea, had babysat and worked summers on neighbouring farms doing housework to help out and pay for her music lessons. Luke, large and strong from the time he was fourteen, did whatever manual labour came his way.

The three children, Neal, Luke and Katherine, had spent all their spare time together, riding their bikes along the country roads, climbing the rocks on the shore, exploring caves, taking out Neal's little sailboat and swimming in all kinds of weather. Katherine closed her eyes and smiled to herself.

'How was it, Katie?' came Barbara's voice. Katherine opened her eyes and glanced over at her. She was sewing buttons on one of Neal's shirts. 'I mean, seeing Luke again.'

Katherine sighed and looked away. 'Not so good,' she finally admitted, sighing again. 'At first I thought he didn't recognise me. I know I've changed, and I'm still going under the name of Croft.' Then she thought of that scene in her house, when he had so cruelly had his revenge. 'But he did,' she added, meeting Barbara's eyes and smiling a little.

'What happened?' Barbara asked, her eyes intent on her sewing.

Katherine stretched. 'It wasn't pleasant. I'll spare you the details, but it was painful for both of us.'

'Does he know about Brian?'

'You mean, that we're no longer married?' Katherine had never discussed the reason for her broken marriage with Barbara, and she wondered now if Neal had ever told her. Barbara nodded, her mouth set in a hard line. 'I suppose so. I hate to give him that satisfaction too. He's already had his revenge.'

Barbara gave her a sharp look, but Katherine was staring out at the water, turning a darker blue now that dusk had fallen.

'How's Jim Hawkins?' Barbara asked casually. 'He hasn't been over here for a long time. Neal and I both like him very much.'

There was a long pause as Katherine thought over her sister-in-law's question. She hated any intrusion on her private life. Luke had temporarily disturbed her equanimity, but that was all over now. All she wanted was to resume her orderly life.

'I like Jim very much,' she said evenly at last. 'He's a good friend, a wonderful boss, but that's all.' She jumped up. 'I think I'll run down to the beach to find Neal and Nancy.'

As she passed by Barbara's chair, she hesitated, then touched her lightly on the shoulder. Barbara looked up with troubled eyes. 'Don't worry about me, Barbara, Really, I'm fine. I like living alone. I'm a confirmed old maid.'

She gave a little laugh, then set off down the sloping path that led to the beach.

CHAPTER FIVE

THE next morning they had breakfast out on the deck. Neal had pulled down the bamboo blinds against the sun. Later that day Barbara and Neal were to drive Nancy up to the northern tip of the island and deposit her for a week at summer camp. It would be the little girl's first stay away from home.

Watching her now across the picnic table, sitting solemn and quiet between her mother and father, her hazel eyes wide, Katherine remembered her first trip away from home, a week spent with her grandmother in Spokane. She recalled how excited she was in the anticipation of spending time away from her family, but also the awful feeling of desolation at the pit of her stomach.

Neal was fussing as usual, on his fifth cigarette and third cup of coffee.

'Now, you're sure you packed everything on the list, Barbara?' he asked. His brow was furrowed, his foot tapping on the deck.

'Yes, Neal,' his wife said calmly. She turned to him and said meekly, 'But I'd feel much better if you checked it again.'

'Good idea,' he said. He jumped to his feet, drained the last of his coffee, snuffed out his cigarette and went off happily.

Barbara and Katherine exchanged a conspiratorial look. Katherine smiled.

'You handle Neal like a master,' she said admiringly. 'He's a lucky man.'

Barbara gave a little laugh, tossed her dark curls and got up to start clearing the table, 'Oh, no,' she said with a secret smile, 'I'm the one who's lucky. Your brother may require a little special—er—diplomacy from time to time, but he gives back far more than he gets.'

Katherine couldn't resist the stab of envy that suddenly pierced her heart. For a moment she felt the dreariness of her life, the long empty years ahead of her, all alone.

Then she noticed the look on Nancy's face as she followed her mother around the table with her eyes. She knew the girl was close to tears at the imminent parting. She rose to her feet.

'Come on, Nancy,' she said, 'let's take the boat out and check the crab pots.' She glanced a question at Barbara, who gave her a grateful look. 'Unless you need me to help, Barbara,' she added.

'No, I can manage. You two run along. Don't forget your lifejacket, Nancy, if you're going out in the boat.'

Hand in hand they walked down the steep path to the beach. Every step along the way was as familiar to Katherine as her own heartbeat. Every tree, every bush, every rock brought back a flood of memories from her own childhood.

At the edge of the shore, where the packed dry earth gradually blended into the sand on the beach, they stopped to take off their shoes. Katherine started to roll up her blue denims.

'Aunt Katie,' Nancy said soberly, 'I don't think I want to look for crabs.' She wrinkled her nose. 'Nasty things!'

Katherine squatted down beside her. 'I don't blame you. I never liked them either.' She straightened up. 'I can't stand cooking them alive, either,' she added. 'But I do like to eat them. Let's just take a walk up the beach and look for shells.'

The little girl skipped ahead, pigtails flying, stooping now and then to examine a shell or pretty rock. She would bring her treasure back to Katherine, they would examine it together, then either discard it as unworthy of the collection or put it in their pants pockets.

Her earlier fears seemed to be forgotten. Katherine knew they would return at the moment of parting from her parents, but at least she wouldn't be spending the whole morning in that agony of apprehension Katherine remembered so well.

It was a gorgeous morning. The sun moved slowly in the eastern sky, warming the golden sand. The waves lapped gently against the shore, leaving a thin edge of white foam before receding again back into the blue water.

By afternoon it would be warm enough to swim, Katherine thought. She was looking forward to some time alone and had declined Neal's invitation to drive to Nancy's camp with them. It would be better, she thought, for the little family to say its first goodbyes alone anyway.

Soon, without realising it until she could actually

see the little brown house set up on a jutting promontory, it dawned on her that they had wandered as far as the old Dillon house.

After Mrs Dillon died, Luke and Althea had sold the house to a retired army officer and his wife. He had died recently, and the wife had gone to live with her married daughter in Portland.

The house looked vacant, with no curtains at the windows or any other sign of life. Katherine stood on the shore looking up at the familiar house, remembering all the times she and Neal had waited down here for Luke to finish his chores so that they could go off on one of their excursions.

Suddenly she became aware of movement at the side of the house, and her heart leaped as a tall figure, dark-headed, with khaki trousers and a white teeshirt, started down the steep path from the house. For a moment, she thought, her hand at her throat, it had looked exactly like Luke as he used to come down to meet her in the old days.

She was about to turn away, not wanting to trespass or intrude, when she realised as the man came closer that it *was* Luke. She caught her breath and held it as he strode slowly towards her across the stretch of sandy beach. The thin cotton knit of his shirt stretched tautly against his broad shoulders and powerful chest muscles. The slim trousers moulded his narrow hips and muscular legs. His crisp dark hair was mussed, falling over his forehead, the deep set eyes quizzical under raised eyebrows. He hadn't shaved yet, and a fine dark stubble darkened his jaw.

'What—what are you doing here?' Katherine

asked as he approached her within a few yards. She
tried to make her voice sound casual and forced out
an icy polite smile.

He folded his arms across his broad chest and
gave her a withering look. 'I might ask you the same
question,' he said frostily. 'Is this your wild
weekend trip? Visiting your brother and his family?'

His cool contemptuous tone irritated her beyond
words. The arrogant male, she thought bitterly, in
all his glory.

'Number one,' she said coldly, 'you jumped to
the conclusion that it was going to be, in your
tactful words, "a wild weekend trip," ' She bit out
each word with contempt. 'Number two, it's none
of your damn business what I do with my
weekends.'

He raised one heavy eyebrow in mock amazement. 'My, my, Mrs Croft—such language! And
with children present!'

Katherine glanced down to see Nancy standing at
her side looking up at her with puzzled eyes.
Katherine flushed and put an arm around the girl's
narrow shoulders, drawing her close.

'Come on, Nancy,' she said, 'we'd better get
back.' She turned to go.

'Wait a minute,' Luke commanded. Against her
will, Katherine slowly turned around. 'Is that
Neal's girl?' he asked in a softer tone. He was
staring down at Nancy, a quirky smile on his thin
mouth.

The girl looked up at Katherine, then shyly stole
a glance at Luke, and one small hand stole into

Katherine's. 'Yes, it is,' she said, clutching Nancy's hand, 'and we're in a hurry.'

He looked at her. 'She's very much like you were as a girl,' he said softly.

Katherine winced, more afraid of his softness than his cruelty. She put her hands on her hips. 'Just what are you doing here, anyway?' she asked angrily.

'Don't worry, I'm not staying,' he said easily. 'I'm thinking of buying the place back now that it's vacant. I'd like to have a summer place in Seattle.'

'You wouldn't!' she breathed. Her heart sank.

'Why ever not?' he asked. He appeared to be genuinely puzzled at her reaction, but Katherine knew him too well not to notice the gleam of devilment in those dark hooded eyes.

'Oh, do what you please,' she snapped. She clutched Nancy's hand more tightly and started back to Neal's. All the way down the beach she had the uneasy sensation that those dark eyes were boring into her so that the skin on her back actually tingled with discomfort. She never once turned around, however, and it wasn't until she and Nancy started up the path to the house that she dared to glance up the beach. He was gone.

Neal, Barbara and Nancy set off for the camp right after lunch. Katherine went out to the driveway with them and waved them out of sight. Nancy had gazed at her through the rear window until the car turned the last bend in the road, the big eyes solemn, the lower lip quivering.

When they were gone, Katherine stood for a moment in the shade of the enormous walnut tree that had been there for as long as she could remember. Though it was loaded with nuts every year, they had never harvested a single one, thanks to the multitude of foraging squirrels on the island. The sun was directly overhead now. It was very warm.

As she slowly turned to go back in the house, she recalled the evening so long ago when Brian had driven her home from the dance, the first night she had ever let him kiss her, hold her in his arms, the night Luke had come home unexpectedly and had waited and watched in the darkness from behind that same walnut tree.

She glanced at it now, half expecting him to leap out at her again as he had that night, his dark eyes murderous, his hands like steel on her arms, his shoulders heaving as he turned from her and walked out of her life for ever.

A squirrel rustled on the branch of the tree, dropped a walnut to the ground and chattered angrily at her, its sharp little nose twitching. She jumped, then smiled at her idiocy. Luke would never come here again, she thought as she started walking towards the house. Besides, he had said he wasn't staying. He was probably back in Seattle by now.

By the time she had cleared the lunch table, put the food away and rinsed the dishes and put them in the dishwasher, she was perspiring. She decided to go for a swim. Tomorrow she'd catch the early ferry back to town and spend the day cleaning her house and working in the garden.

She went up to her room to change into the cream-coloured bikini that set off her deep golden hair and tan, grabbed a beach towel and headed down the path to the deserted beach.

Before she could lose her nerve she plunged into the water, gasping a little at its icy coldness. She floated about lazily for a while, buoyed up by the salt water, then struck out with strong even strokes across the little bay to the rock promontory to the south. She swam back slowly, exhausted by the swim, but invigorated at the same time from the cold water.

She stepped out of the water, gasping and dripping. She moved the beach towel over to a spot where she knew it would be shady in less than half an hour and lay face down on it, first unpinning her hair so it would dry faster. She closed her eyes and immediately drifted into a half-sleep, where her thoughts wandered freely with an eerie dreamlike quality.

She found herself thinking of Brian Croft, of all things, her partner in that ridiculous, short-lived marriage. She hadn't thought of him in years. She had no idea where he was, and she didn't really care. She had never loved him and it never occurred to her to wonder whether or not he had really loved her in his way. He had begged her to marry him. Luke was out of her life for good, torn from her like a leg or an arm, leaving only a bleeding stump behind.

Still, Brian had been her husband, and she had decided she would try to be a good wife to him in every sense of the word. He was sweet, gentle, considerate, good-looking, all any girl could ask for. It wasn't until their wedding night that he had faced her in tears with his dreadful secret. She would never forget the look on his face as he begged her forgiveness, pleaded with her to stay with him.

She shuddered a little in her trance at the memory of that awful night, her quick flight back to her parents' house, the weeks of discussions between the families, and finally a quiet divorce. At least she had given him that. An annulment would have aired the whole messy business.

She drifted now into a real sleep as the shadows closed in on her, sheltering her from the burning sun. She dreamed of Luke, as he was when they were so close. In the dream she was lying on the beach with his long hard frame beside her, stroking her back, rubbing suntan oil over her shoulders and down her spine so she wouldn't burn.

She smiled in her sleep and made a little moan of pleasure at his touch. Then, gradually, she began to wake up, and it wasn't a dream. There was a real hand, large and firm, moving caressingly over her back, across her shoulders, under her hair to knead her neck gently.

She opened one eye and saw an expanse of bronzed flesh, hard thigh muscles under dark blue bathing trunks. She opened the eye wider to see Luke, bare-chested, sitting beside her, facing her, his eyes half-closed, a brooding look on his face.

She turned slowly on her side and propped herself up on one elbow, facing him, still half asleep. His hand was resting lightly on her bare waist.

Sleepily, she watched him as his gaze travelled to the skimpy bra of her bikini, which revealed most of the soft rounded white flesh beneath. He reached out a hand and gathered up a handful of her flowing hair. Their eyes met in a long, searching, yearning gaze.

Then he leaned over. Katherine's eyes grew wider as the familiar face came closer and closer. Then she shut them as his mouth found hers. The pressure of his lips insistently propelled her head and shoulders around until she lay flat on her back.

Gently but imperiously his mouth moved on hers until her lips parted and then seemed to melt. Her whole body was suffused with warmth. Only his mouth on hers existed. Slowly, still drinking in her kiss, Luke stretched out beside her so that their legs met along their whole length, and she shuddered as she felt the rough hair on his legs against her smooth ones.

Then he tore his mouth from hers and, resting the weight of his upper body on hers, buried his head in her hair, his hot breath panting into her ear.

'Ah, Katie,' he whispered. 'My Katie!'

Her arms went around his neck and she dug her hands into the hard muscles of his shoulders and back, stroking and caressing until he groaned aloud. He lifted his head and propped himself up on one elbow to gaze deeply into her eyes.

With their eyes locked together he put a hand on her cheek, his thumb brushing her lips. Her body was on fire. Luke moved his hand down to her throat, then her shoulder. His gaze lowered and at the same time she felt his hand gently close on her half bare breast, straining now almost out of the skimpy bra. She moaned and closed her eyes as he untied the front opening and moulded the outline of each full white breast, teasing the nipples until she ached with longing.

He lowered his head to her body and with his hand kneading one breast, he took the taut nipple of the other in his mouth, kissing and licking until she thought she would go mad. She clutched at his head, her hands buried in the thick black hair. With his mouth still on her breast, his hand moved now downward, across her abdomen to the edge of the brief elastic top of her bikini, then slid slowly to her thighs.

She could feel the hardness of his body next to her, pressing against her leg. His mouth came back to her face and kissed her deeply, his mouth engulfing hers, warm and demanding.

Then, in strong arms, he lifted her. She felt her bikini top slip from her shoulders as she threw her head back. He carried her up the path to the house, while she clung to him, her bare breasts crushed against his chest, their mouths still drinking each other in.

Just as they reached the top of the hill and he had kicked open the door to the kitchen, Katherine slowly began to come to her senses. Something about the whole situation, the two of them, almost naked, here in her old home, the scene of so much that was painful about the past, suddenly jolted her awake to the stark fact of the crazy thing she was doing.

She tensed in his grasp, her body stiffening away

from him. She thought of that night at her house, when Luke's hands and mouth had aroused her to almost this same pitch of desire and then had withdrawn so abruptly. She saw again his mocking eyes and cruel smile, reading in them the desire to humiliate her, to wreak his revenge for a ten-year-old hurt. He would never change. He was like a rock, implacable. She had wounded his ego so deeply he would never forgive her.

'Put me down!' she cried. As he gazed at her in amazement, she started pounding on his chest. 'Put me down!' she screamed.

Wordlessly, he obeyed, and Katherine covered her naked breasts with her hands, trembling. Her body had betrayed her for the last time, she vowed. He reached out a hand toward her. She drew back.

'What's the matter, Luke?' she spat at him. 'Wasn't once enough? Did you have to take your revenge twice?' He only stared at her, white-faced, his jaw set, his eyes narrowed. 'Get out!' she cried.

He ran contemptuous eyes over her near-naked body, then, without a word, turned and left the house.

On Sunday morning Katherine took the early ferry back to Seattle, as she had planned. She had the distinct impression that Neal and Barbara, free for the first time since Nancy was born, were not sorry to see her go. She was well aware of the lingering looks that passed between them, the way they touched or brushed up against each other, and she realised that their marriage was not quite as stodgy as she had imagined.

Her little house seemed like an oasis of serenity and peace after the steamy erotic atmosphere on Bainbridge Island. She spent the day as usual, cleaning and gardening and getting her clothes ready for the work week ahead.

In spite of all the activity—she made herself do jobs she had been putting off for weeks—she continually caught herself during the day going over and over the scene with Luke on the beach. As she washed a window, gradually her movements would get slower and slower until she found herself wiping the same spot for minutes at a time, once again feeling Luke's mouth on hers, his hands roaming possessively over her body, the aching agony of desire she had felt for him.

'Why did he have to come back into my life?' she asked aloud as she scrubbed the bathtub until it gleamed. Later she found herself banging the iron down so hard on her new silk blouse that she scorched it.

Of course, she wondered what would have happened if she had given in to her feelings, allowed Luke to carry her up to her bedroom to take full possession of her. Angrily, she dumped rubbish in the garbage can and slammed down the lid. She knew what would have happened. It would merely have been another opportunity for him to reject her. She would never forget the look of triumph and contempt on his face that night.

By the time she fell, exhausted, into bed late Sunday night, she had firmly determined her future course of action. She had to work with Luke Dillon and she'd have to go through with it, but from now on it would be all business between them. She'd leave her job before she'd ever let him lay a hand on her again.

The next morning the phone rang just as Katherine started out the door. She hesitated, tempted not to answer it. She was running late and would miss her bus if she didn't hurry. Then, impulsively, as if happy to forestall her meeting with Luke, she set down her purse and went back into the house.

'Hi, Katherine,' came Jim's cheerful voice. 'Glad I caught you.'

'Jim!' she exclaimed, delighted to hear his voice, so safe and secure, 'I thought you were going out of town today for a deposition.'

'That's why I called. I have to go to Yakima for the dep and I can't get a court reporter. I thought you might like to go along and try your hand.'

'Oh, Jim, I don't think I'm good enough. I'd miss half of it.'

'No problem. We'll take along a tape recorder and you can transcribe from it later if you miss anything.'

She hesitated, thinking about the few pages of untranscribed notes at the office for Luke's reply to the summary judgement motion. There were still almost three weeks before it needed to be served and filed. Besides, she welcomed the opportunity to avoid Luke.

'Well,' she began, 'if you think I can do it . . .'

He chuckled delightedly. 'Good girl! I'll be by the house to pick you up in ten minutes. Why don't you call the office and let Sharon know where we'll be.'

Katherine did as he asked, resisting the impulse to tell her to let Luke know. Let him fret, she decided. Jim Hawkins was her boss. She brushed aside a nagging feeling of guilt. It wasn't an emergency, after all.

Jim watched her as she came down the path towards the car, his eyes bright with appreciation. She had on a white accordion-pleated skirt, a black and white print blouse with a little tie at the neck, and her white linen jacket.

He leaned over to open the door for her. 'You look good enough to eat,' he said with a grin. He touched her cheek and grazed her lips lightly with his own. His mouth was cool and dry.

'Thank you, sir,' she replied as he put the car in gear and drove off. 'It's been ages since I've been east of the mountains. I'll bet it's like a furnace over there.'

They headed south on the freeway, across the Mercer Island floating bridge, set on pontoons across Lake Washington, and started climbing towards Snoqualmie Pass.

The Cascade Mountains cut the states of Washington and Oregon in half so that east and west of them are like two separate states. The western half is cool and damp, with heavy ever-green forestation, lakes and streams, and a mild temperature. The eastern half is dry and barren, with summer and winter extremes of temperature.

As they passed over the mountain summit and started down the other side, the vegetation became sparser, the road flatter and the temperature rose up past ninety degrees.

'Actually,' Jim was explaining, 'this isn't a very important deposition—just a retired minor official of one of the lumber companies. All I want from him is an admission that on a certain day three years ago he received a certain phone call.'

'And what will that prove?' Katherine asked.

They had both taken off their jackets. Jim's short-sleeved blue shirt fluttered around his tanned upper arm in the breeze through the open window.

'I hope, collusion with the other lumber companies to fix prices,' he replied. 'That is, if I can get him to say what I want him to say.'

He gave her a quick smile, then turned his eyes back to the road. Katherine watched him as he concentrated on his driving, his eyes narrowed against the glare of the sun. His profile was pleasant, clean-cut, with a straight nose and fuller mouth than Luke's. His light brown hair was blown off his forehead. Katherine smiled with contentment and leaned back in the seat. Jim always made her feel so comfortable.

'Why are you smiling?' he asked.

'Oh, I don't know.' She stretched her legs, cramped from sitting in one position for so long.

He reached out a hand and rested it lightly on her knee. 'I like to see you smile,' he said lightly. 'You don't do it nearly enough.'

Katherine looked down at his hand, square, well-manicured, with a light mat of blondish hair on the back and on his bare arm. She wondered if she should tell him about her past association with

Luke, confide her awkward present situation to him.

Jim gave her knee a little squeeze, then withdrew his hand. 'You know how I feel about you, Katherine,' he said in a low voice. He gave her a quick glance. His clear blue eyes were so direct, she thought, so guileless. Not like Luke's burning dark ones, so deep-set, with the black brows hovering over them so that he appeared to be angry and brooding even when he wore one of his rare smiles.

'Jim—' she began, touching his arm lightly.

'I know,' he said. 'I won't push. One of these days you'll drop the mask and tell me about the real Katherine Croft. That's all I'm waiting for.'

The real Katherine Croft, she thought with dismay. He'd never believe it.

'Here we are,' Jim said at last. 'Beautiful downtown Yakima, the fruit bowl of the North-west!'

They turned off the interstate on to the narrow road that led into the small city. On either side, as far as the eye could see, were rows and rows of fruit trees—apples, cherries, peaches, pears, apricots.

It took Jim exactly one hour to get the admission he wanted from the witness, a vigorous and independent old man who had no love for the company that had forcibly retired him in what he considered to be the prime of his life.

The company's attorney was distraught and kept objecting to statements made by his own client. But Jim skilfully guided the old man exactly where he wanted him to go.

'And so, Mr Bennett,' he said at last, 'for the record, would you say that this conference call of

May the eighteenth,1977, between the four defendants, in which you took part, constituted an
attempt to fix prices of raw lumber?'

'Hell, yes!' roared Mr Bennett, a great bear of a
man with a thatch of unruly white hair and gigantic
hands. He kept thumping them on the table whenever he wanted to make a point.

Katherine, her pencil racing on the pad to get it
all down, could barely suppress a giggle. Mr Bennett's attorney was livid, purple and sputtering with
rage.

When it was all over the three men stood chatting
amicably while Katherine gathered up the exhibits
which she had carefully marked and numbered.
She was filled with wonder at the way men could be
shouting at each other one minute and shaking
hands and joking together the next.

She mentioned this to Jim as they walked to the
car. He looked at her in surprise.

'You should know by now that the law is only a
game,' he said as he opened the car door for her.
His fingers brushed against her shoulder as she slid
into the seat. 'No reason to hold a grudge over a
game,' he added as he got behind the wheel. He
shrugged and started the engine. 'You win a few,
lose a few. It's just a game.'

'Yes,' she said wryly, 'and a very expensive one,
with millions of dollars at stake.'

'Oh, there's that, too,' he said as they drove off.
'But that's what makes it interesting.'

She sighed. She would never understand why
men got so much pleasure out of dangerous games.
Women want security, men want risk. Then she

thought of Selma Boyd-Richards, who seemed to want both—and would probably get it, too.

They stopped in Yakima for a leisurely lunch. Jim was good company. He liked to discuss his cases with her, unlike many lawyers who seemed to go out of their way to keep their business a secret from their secretaries. Katherine knew it made her job more interesting to know what was going on, as well as making her more valuable to Jim and better able to help him.

They arrived back in Seattle by three o'clock. Jim let her off in front of the building while he parked the car. As she rode up in the elevator to the fifteenth floor, she began to feel pangs of guilt about her truancy. Her heartbeat began to jump crazily in anticipation of facing Luke. Her knees felt weak and she clutched her handbag so tightly that her knuckles were white.

She smiled at Sharon, manning the reception desk. 'Any problems?' she asked lightly.

Sharon rolled her eyes, sucked in her cheeks and beckoned her with one hand. Katherine leaned over the counter.

'Dillon's been asking for you all day,' Sharon hissed at her. 'He's been snapping everybody's head off. You'd better go see what he wants.'

Katherine set her jaw firmly. 'Mr Dillon doesn't scare me. He can't fire me, and he can only kill me once.'

'That's the spirit!' Sharon whispered. 'Good luck.'

Katherine almost collided with Irene Connors as she turned the corner into the corridor. The tall willowy blonde glared at her.

'That man!' she spat angrily. 'Where have you been?' Without waiting for a reply, she went on, 'I've been working my tail off for him all day and *nothing* satisfies him. Not even a thank you, Irene. What a beast!'

Katherine sighed. 'I'm truly sorry, Irene. I had to go on a dep with Jim. It's too bad you got stuck with the abominable snowman.'

'Miss Croft,' came a curt deep voice behind her.

Irene scurried off and Katherine whirled around to face a livid Luke Dillon.

'Just where the hell have you been all day?' he barked at her.

'I've been working,' she said coldly. 'For *my* boss. Didn't Sharon tell you?' She turned from him and started off down the hall to her desk.

He followed her. 'You knew I needed that draft reply today. Why didn't you finish it on Friday night?'

'I explained that to you then,' Katherine replied. She walked on, head held high, eyes straight ahead. 'You don't own me, you know. You're not my employer.'

'Well, thank God for that!' he breathed.

They had reached her desk. Katherine was aware of Teresa's fascinated gaze. Slowly, she set her notebook and handbag down on the desk and turned to him. 'You had help,' she said. 'Irene's a good secretary.'

He gestured angrily at her notebook. 'Sure she is, but a genius couldn't decipher those chicken scratches.'

Katherine flushed guiltily. He had a point. She had had to write so fast to keep up with his dictation that only she could make out the short cuts she had taken.

'Look,' she said, 'I'm sorry, but Jim needed me. You've got almost three weeks to serve and file the reply. I'll get on it right away and have it for you in an hour—maybe less if you leave me alone.'

He looked her up and down insultingly. 'Oh, don't ever worry about that,' he said, his thin mouth curled in contempt. 'I'll never bother you again that way.'

Katherine flushed deeply and had to look away. In spite of all her effort of will, she couldn't help remembering the feel of his hand on her bare skin, his hot kisses and hard body pressed close to her.

'Well, I'm grateful for that, anyway,' she murmured.

'Yes,' he said bitterly so only she could hear, 'you should be very pleased with yourself to have stabbed the same man in the gut twice in one lifetime.'

He turned and left. Katherine sat down at her desk and with trembling fingers uncovered her typewriter and began to fumble in her notebook for Friday's notes.

What did he mean, she wondered, twice in one lifetime? How dared he accuse her of anything after the way he had humiliated her? Her self-righteous anger calmed her nerves and she started typing, oblivious to Teresa's stare boring into her back, oblivious to everything but getting the words down on paper so he'd leave her alone.

She had just finished the last page and was looking through them for errors when she saw Selma go into Luke's office and shut the door. Damn, she thought, I don't want to go in there now. But still, she had promised to get the pages to him as soon as possible.

She shuffled the papers into a neat pile, got up and walked over to his office. She stood at the door for a moment, listening. There was a dead silence, then a muffled laugh. Katherine's face grew warm as her imagination painted pictures in her mind of the scene behind the closed door.

Then she thought, what do I care? He said he wanted the draft as soon as I was through, and that's what he'll get. She raised her hand to knock out a warning before going in, when the door opened.

She felt like a fool standing there with one hand raised in the air. She dropped it awkwardly to her side and held out the sheaf of papers.

'Here,' she said. 'I've finished.'

Luke was grinning at Selma, and she was glancing sideways at him with adoring eyes. He was in his shirtsleeves, his lightweight tan jacket slung over one shoulder, one hand under Selma's bare elbow.

He flicked a bored look at Katherine from under hooded eyelids. 'Just put it on my desk, will you, Miss Croft?' he said absently. 'I'll look at it tomorrow.'

He propelled Selma past Katherine and they went off down the hall together. Selma was a tall woman, but still her flaming red head only reached to his chin. Katherine stood looking after them, churning with conflicting feelings, half furious that she had worked so hard for nothing and half a yawning chasm of emptiness that she fought down until all she knew was hatred of that cruel, arrogant man.

CHAPTER SIX

THE following weeks passed by quickly in a flurry of activity on the paper case. Luke had won the summary judgment motion against him, which meant that there was indeed a case at law in the opinion of the judge. The next step would probably be settlement negotiations.

Katherine worked long hours every day and many weekends, but she thrived on it. Jim was still gone from the office most of the time on out-of-town discovery, and Luke was preparing all the substantive motions, leaving interrogatories and requests for production of documents up to Selma.

As time passed, and Katherine found more and more responsibility handed to her by all three lawyers, she soon became indispensable to them, and she knew it. The feeling of being part of a well organised team, captained by the demanding, tireless, indefatigable Luke, was exhilarating to her.

It was soon discovered that she was the only one of the four who could ever put her hands on exactly the document or letter they were looking for, and all three of them came to her from then on before even attempting to find it themselves.

Her admiration for Luke's legal capabilities grew daily. Once they had arrived at an armed truce and plunged into their intense involvement in the case, all personal animosity was forgotten. Katherine even learned a grudging respect for Selma's ability to get things done.

Teresa's boss was on vacation during the whole month of August, and her help had been invaluable to Katherine. She was a fast and accurate typist, willing to work overtime when necessary, and she now typed up all the deposition summaries and did all the other odd jobs Katherine was too busy to handle.

On a Friday afternoon in early September, Katherine was rushing to get a brief typed for service that day when Selma came running out of Luke's office.

'Katherine, we've got to get these four subpoenas typed and issued right away so I can serve them at the five o'clock meeting.'

'Oh, Lord, Selma,' Katherine groaned, 'I can't do it. I still have four more pages of this brief.' She looked over at Teresa. 'Teresa?'

'Okay, okay,' Teresa answered, 'but it's Friday and I want to get out of here on time.'

Selma took the blank subpoena forms over to her. 'Thanks a million, Teresa. Here's all the information. I'll run up to federal court to get them signed by the clerk the minute you're through.'

'You know,' Teresa remarked after Selma had gone, 'that girl is becoming almost human. Makes me think lady lawyers aren't so bad after all.'

Katherine murmured absently and continued typing. Teresa rolled the first subpoena form into her typewriter.

'I think our friendly leader, Luke Dillon, has had

a lot to do with her improvement in personality,' she remarked.

Katherine stopped typing and turned to face her. 'What in the world are you talking about?'

'Hadn't you noticed? She's crazy about him. I must say I don't think he finds her actually repulsive.' Teresa typed for a few minutes, then stopped. 'However, he doesn't look at her the way he does you.'

Katherine's eyes widened. 'If you're saying what I think you're saying,' she stated firmly, 'you couldn't be more mistaken.'

'Oh, really? Well, if you say so. I'll tell you, though, if a man like Luke Dillon gave me one of those brooding, hungry looks, I'd be mighty tempted to put one over on Tony!'

Katherine laughed scornfully and went back to her brief. Teresa finished the subpoenas in half an hour and stopped at Katherine's desk on her way to Luke's office. She leaned down so that her eyes were on a level with Katherine's.

'Do you suppose,' she asked with a little nod in the direction of the office, 'that they're sleeping together?'

'Oh, Teresa, for heaven's sake, how should I know? I doubt it. Selma's married.'

'Oh, sure,' Teresa snorted, 'some marriage! I'd like to catch Tony trying to pull an open marriage on me! What kind of marriage is that?'

'Well, I'll admit it's not my cup of tea,' Katherine replied, 'but there's no disputing tastes, as the saying goes.'

'You know, Katherine, if you'd give Luke Dillon

any kind of encouragement . . .'

'Forget it, Teresa. I'm not interested and neither is he. Come on, now, I've got to get this brief done.'

In spite of all the odds against it, she did finish the brief by four o'clock. Luke read it over carefully and signed it, Katherine made the copies, and Teresa volunteered to serve it and file it on her way home.

'I can do that in fifteen minutes,' she said, 'then I can catch my early bus.' She gathered up the package of documents. 'See you Monday,' she called as she set off down the hall.

'Have a nice weekend,' Katherine called after her.

She saw Selma rush off a few minutes later, subpoenas in hand. She looked at the untidy mess on her desk and sighed. By the time she straightened it up and got the office copy of the brief safely filed away, it was after five. As always on a Friday afternoon, the office was deserted.

Katherine gathered up her handbag and light weight jacket and slowly set off down the hall to the elevators. She was ineffably weary. Every bone and muscle ached, her head throbbed, and she recognised the onset of the familiar letdown that always came after a day like today when she managed to do the near impossible under intolerable pressure through sheer effort of will and nervous energy.

There wasn't a soul in the office. Even Sharon had gone home. That's odd, Katherine thought, as she passed by the coffee room. Sharon always locked up when she left unless a lawyer was still working. Then she heard noises coming from the coffee room, the sound of running water, a heavy bang, the breaking of glass and a series of loud curses.

Luke appeared at the door to the coffee room, a broken pyrex coffee pot in one hand, the other bound up with a handkerchief. The white material was slowly turning red. Katherine looked at him. His hair was dishevelled, his tie askew, his eyes wild and his face as white as the handkerchief.

'I need some help,' he croaked pitifully.

Katherine set her bag and jacket down on the counter of the reception desk and went quickly to his side. 'What in the world have you done?' she asked.

He held out his hand. The handkerchief was now soaked with blood. 'What have *I* done?' he asked with an injured air. 'I haven't done anything. The question is, what clown left an empty coffee pot on the burner? When I picked it up and ran water in it, the damn thing exploded!'

'What are you doing making coffee at five-thirty anyway?' she asked.

'Don't ask stupid questions!' he bellowed, poking his bleeding hand in her face, '*do* something!' His voice faltered. 'I can't stand the sight of my own blood.'

Katherine half guided, half pushed him over to a chair in the coffee room. She rummaged in the cupboard under the sink until she found the first aid kit. She set several paper towels down on the table where Luke was sitting and told him to set his arm down on them. She unbuttoned his shirt at the cuff and rolled up the sleeve to his elbow. Then she soaked a large cotton pad in disinfectant, took away the bloody handkerchief and gently began to swab the injured hand so she could see just how badly he was cut.

'Ouch!' he roared. 'That hurts!' He gave her an accusing look.

'Oh, for heaven's sake,' Katherine said disgustedly, 'of course it hurts.' Now she could see the cut, just below his wrist. It wasn't deep enough for stitches, she decided. She taped it tightly shut and began wrapping gauze around his wrist. 'You always were a baby about the sight of blood,' she muttered as she worked.

'Only my own,' he said through clenched teeth. 'I can recall bandaging many a bloody knee for you.'

She smiled to herself, remembering. He was right. She tied the gauze neatly and surveyed her handiwork. 'There,' she said, 'that should stop the bleeding. I don't think you'll need stitches.'

'I sincerely hope not,' he said dryly, gazing warily at the bandage for signs of blood. He flexed his wrist, turning it this way and that.

'You act like you expect it to fall off any minute,' Katherine remarked, unable to suppress a smile of amusement.

Luke glared at her. Then the muscles of his face relaxed, his eyes softened and his thin mouth began to twitch.

'All right,' he sighed, 'you win. You know my weaknesses too well.' He leaned his broad shoulders back in the chair and spread his legs out in front of him. 'God, I'm tired,' he said. He put a hand on his forehead.

Katherine stood up. 'I'm not surprised,' she remarked tartly. She began to put the gauze and adhesive back in the first aid kit. 'I'll have to admit you drive yourself at least as hard as you do your slaves.'

He darted a quick look at her. 'I know how hard you've been working,' he said quietly. 'I appreciate it. I couldn't have managed without you.'

Their eyes met briefly, then Katherine looked away. 'Well,' she said lightly, 'thank you, sir. Coming from you that's high praise.' She walked over to the sink and put the first aid kit back in the cupboard.

'What do you hear from Jim?' he asked her.

'He's working hard, too,' she replied. She started to clear up the broken glass from the counter. 'Tired of travelling.'

'You and he don't see much of each other these days, I take it.'

'Hardly,' she said. She finished mopping the counter and turned to him. He was examining the bandage on his wrist.

'Would you mind taking another look at this?' he asked. 'It feels like it's seeping.'

She took his hand in hers and tested the bandage to see if it was secure. 'It's good and tight,' she said. 'No sign of blood.' His hand was in hers, palm up, and she was suddenly intensely aware of the feel of his skin against hers, the silky hairs on the back of his hand, the bones and muscles of his arm. She glanced up at the strong muscles of his inner arm, the skin softer there, a large blue vein running down it.

'Would you like me to button your shirt?' she asked in a low voice.

'Please,' he said. Katherine rolled his sleeve down carefully over the bandage and buttoned his cuff. He looked up at her. 'Are you going to marry Jim, Katie?' he asked softly.

She stiffened. 'Why do you ask?' She let go his hand and moved a step back from him.

'No reason,' he said casually. He stood up, towering over her. 'Just curious. He's a good guy, you could do a lot worse.'

'You mean as I once did?' she asked. Her voice was brittle and she shot him a challenging look.

His eyes widened. 'No, that isn't what I meant,' he said slowly. He looked down at her. 'I don't know what happened between you and Brian. I never wanted to know.'

Katherine laughed shortly and turned away. 'Nothing happened,' she said, and was appalled to feel tears stinging her eyes. 'That was the trouble.'

There was silence between them as Luke digested this bit of information and Katherine struggled for control. Finally, without looking directly at him, she turned.

'Well,' she said brightly, 'I'm off. I wouldn't play handball or punch anybody with that hand for a while or the bleeding might start in again.'

'I'll ride down with you,' he said.

'I thought you were going to work some more?'

'I was,' Luke replied, falling into step beside her. He raised his injured hand. 'But this has destroyed my mood.'

He locked the door to the office behind them and

they rode down in the elevator together in silence. Luke seemed thoughtful, withdrawn, a frown of concentration on his face. Glancing at him out of the corner of her eye, Katherine wondered what was going through his mind. The angle of his jaw, the planes of his flat cheekbones, those deep set dark eyes were so close she could have reached up and touched them. His navy blue jacket was hanging over one arm, his injured hand in his trousers pocket.

She turned to him as they stepped out of the elevator. The lobby of the building was nearly deserted.

'Well, have a nice weekend,' she said. 'I presume you'll be working.'

'As a matter of fact, I'm not.' He hesitated a second. 'I'm going up to Orcas Island tonight to see Althea.' They were out on the sidewalk now. 'She has a summer place up in the San Juan Islands. I'm going to spend the weekend with her. She's singing in the opening opera of the season in a few weeks, then will go on tour.'

Katherine started walking towards her bus stop. Luke followed along. 'How is your sister?' she asked. 'I didn't even know she was still in the area. I always admired her very much.'

Althea Dillon, almost ten years older than Katherine, had been her childhood ideal. She was extremely talented musically, and some of Katherine's happiest memories were of hearing her play and sing. She was beginning to make a name for herself in operatic circles as a promising mezzo-soprano.

'She's doing very well, I hear,' Katherine remarked.

They were walking down the sidewalk to the bus stop. It was almost six o'clock and the rush hour crowd had dispersed. Katherine found it very natural and even pleasant to be walking by Luke's side. He moved gracefully and easily, like the fine athlete he was, shortening his long strides so that she could keep up with him, just as he had when they were children.

'Yes,' he replied as they crossed the street, 'she's got more offers than she can handle now.' There was pride in his voice. Katherine remembered that he and his sister, working so hard as children, had been very close. Struggle toward a common goal did that to people, she thought. Even she and Luke had set aside their hostilities for the sake of the lawsuit they were both so involved with.

'Well,' she said, 'here's my bus stop.' She waited for him to go, but he still stood there beside her, his eyes squinting into the sun. He looked down at her.

'Come on,' he said brusquely, 'I'll give you a ride home.'

She hesitated. Since that last awful scene on the beach at her brother's house, not a hint of any personal feeling had passed between them. They had established a splendid working relationship. She didn't want anything to spoil it.

She looked up at him with troubled eyes, and he took her arm lightly. 'Come on,' he urged. 'I promise not to attack you.' He grinned. 'Besides, I have an ulterior motive.' He held up his injured arm. 'I may need some first aid on the way home.'

Katherine smiled at him. 'In that case,' she said, 'how can I refuse?'

The Friday night traffic was horrendous. They were stalled three times on the freeway. Once again Katherine marvelled at how well this impulsive and quick-tempered man managed to keep himself under control in a frustrating situation. She could tell the delays annoyed him by the little pulse that throbbed along his jawline and the way his fingers tapped on the steering wheel, but outwardly he seemed imperturbable.

When they pulled up in front of her little house, she turned to thank him and found him looking at her with a thoughtful expression.

'Got any big plans for the weekend?' he asked casually.

'Not really. The usual work in the house and garden.'

'Jim out of town?' She nodded. 'Come with me to Althea's, then,' he said. 'I know she'd like to see you again.'

'Oh, I couldn't,' she demurred instantly.

Luke raised a black eyebrow. 'Why not?'

'Well, I don't know. I can't just barge in on her like that uninvited.'

'Don't worry about that. She always tells me to bring someone when I come.'

Katherine wondered if he'd ever taken Selma up there and if such a thing was allowed in an open marriage.

He reached an arm across in front of her and opened her door. 'Go on,' he urged. 'Throw a few things in a suitcase. We'll grab a bite to eat in

Anacortes.' Still she hesitated. 'Go on,' he insisted.

'Well, if you're sure . . .' She was tempted.

'I'm sure.'

As Katherine packed and changed her clothes, she wondered what in the world had possessed her to say she'd go to Althea's with Luke. She still didn't trust him. His memory of past hurts was too long. Granted, they got along all right now at the office, but Katherine was convinced that was only because of the constant pressure of the job to be done and the fact that they neither saw nor spoke to each other outside the office.

As she slipped on white sharkskin pants and a brown and white striped knit shirt, she almost decided not to go. She had nothing to gain, in that there was certainly no future for her where Luke was concerned, and everything to lose, because conflict with him now on a personal level could jeopardise the precarious balance of their work together at the office.

Not only that, she thought grimly as she snapped the suitcase shut and grabbed a brown sweater, but she didn't trust Luke an inch. If she knew him, he was just waiting for an opportunity to humiliate her again, to taste once more the sweet flavour of revenge.

Then why am I going? she asked herself. She stood helplessly in the middle of her bedroom, the suitcase on the bed, her sweater over her shoulders. She sighed. I'm going, she decided, trying to be honest with herself, for the same reason a moth is drawn to a flame. Part blind instinct, part curiosity, part boredom with the daily routine, and part just wanting to get away and relax.

As she locked the front door behind her and started out to the car, she made a mental promise to herself to be on her guard against Luke, suspicious of his every move. She knew him so well, probably better than anyone else on earth, and was quite sure that he would be looking for another opportunity to get even with her for the past.

Luke was leaning back smoking a cigarette when she opened the door and got in the car. His long legs were sprawled out, his elbow on the open window. He flicked his eyes briefly at her, a quick glance up and down, put out his cigarette in the ashtray on the dashboard, and they drove off.

'It's only about an hour to Anacortes,' he remarked as they entered the freeway. 'We'll miss the seven o'clock ferry, but Althea's not expecting me for dinner. We can grab a bite in Anacortes while we're waiting for the next ferry.'

'Does Althea live alone?' Katherine asked as they drove along.

He glanced at her. 'Yes,' he said shortly. 'Like you, she only finds men an unwelcome intrusion. Marriage would interfere with her career.'

Katherine flushed at the innuendo, but was determined not to rise to the bait.

'You don't approve?' she asked lightly.

Luke glanced at her briefly, one eyebrow raised. 'It's not for me to approve or disapprove. It's her life. I understand the drive that motivates her. She has a great talent and she made the decision to sacrifice other things to develop it. I respect that.'

As they sped northward on the interstate, Katherine felt herself gradually relax. She leaned back in the seat and let the warm air blow on her face through the open window. All the kinks of the terrible day at work began to loosen. Her hair was securely pinned at the back of her head, but a few stray wisps were blown about by the breeze.

In spite of their past quarrels, Katherine felt very much at home with Luke, as only one can with someone known from childhood. Old, old acquaintances become strangely like one's hands or feet, so familiar one isn't really aware of them as separate identities. Luke, always silent unless he had something to say, drove on, smoking occasionally, his eyes on the road. He drove easily and expertly. She closed her eyes.

She woke up when she felt the car stop and heard Luke switch off the motor. She opened her eyes sleepily. It was dark out, but they were parked in a business district and the glow from the street lights and shop windows cast some light into the car.

As she glanced around in that first moment of disorientation on waking in a strange place, she became aware of Luke's gaze on her. His face was almost hidden in the dim light. He looked so angry, she thought, and a little stab of fear clutched at her heart. Then she came fully awake, and the look was gone. There was only a bland mask to replace it.

'You were really out,' he remarked casually, his tone light. 'Hungry?'

'Starving,' she said, suddenly realising just how hungry she was. She looked around. 'Are we in Anacortes already?'

'Yes,' he said shortly. 'Let's go. We only have half an hour before the next ferry to the San Juan Islands.'

They sat at the counter of a diner near the ferry dock and wolfed down hamburgers and coffee. They just made the ferry in time.

It had been years since Katherine had been on a ferry at night, and she was entranced. The water across the straits was as calm as glass, the only sign of life in the dark expanse that surrounded them the blinking lights of the night fishing boats and an occasional buoy.

She and Luke leaned against the railing on the top deck looking out over the straits. It was like being on another planet, Katherine thought, their isolation from the bustle of the city and the pressures of the job almost complete. There were only a few scattered passengers, and they had the deck virtually to themselves.

Finally, Luke broke the silence. His voice was low, his tone subdued. 'There's nothing like it, is there?' he said. 'Makes me wonder what I'm doing beating my brains out practising cut-throat law.'

'You'd never be happy any other way,' Katherine said flatly. 'You thrive on warfare, pitting your wits against an opponent. Jim says the law is all a game.'

'Jim's right,' he said. 'But sometimes you do wonder if it's worth it.'

'Well, there's also the small matter of eating,' she remarked drily. 'Or have you become suddenly independently wealthy?'

He gave her a strange look, then glanced away.

'Oh, that's no problem,' he remarked offhandedly. 'My ambition was to be a partner in a top law firm by the time I was thirty and to be rich before I was thirty-five. I'm already a partner in the best firm in New York, and the money goes with it. I've been put on to some good investments through the contacts I've made. I could retire if I wanted to.'

Katherine believed him. There wasn't a hint of bragging in his tone; he was merely stating facts. That was Luke all over, she thought, see what you want and go after it and assume you'll get it. She shivered a little.

'Cold?' he asked, glancing down at her.

They were standing so close that she could feel the material of his jacket on her bare arm. 'A little,' she said. She was carrying her sweater and started to put it on. Her arms became tangled in the sleeves.

'Here,' said Luke, 'can't you even get dressed by yourself?'

Katherine was about to make a sharp retort when she felt his strong arm encircle her as he helped her into the sweater. He left his arm hanging loosely over her shoulders, one hand dangling dangerously near her breast. Her head started to whirl.

In a moment, she thought crazily, I will feel that hand on my breast. I will turn my head toward him and he will kiss me. She could feel the warmth from his body, smell the scent of his skin, hear the ticking of his watch in the stillness.

Just then, the ship's bell started to clang, and the spell was broken. Luke removed his arm and lit a cigarette. The ferry gradually slowed down. Ahead and to the sides, Katherine could make out large dark shapes in the water. They had reached the islands.

The harbour of Orcas Island was just ahead. Lights flickered along the pier to guide the ferry to its berth, and Katherine and Luke went down to the car. The ferry scraped and bumped against the wooden pilings. There were shouts from the harbourmaster to the ferry engineers, the clanking of chains. The ferry tooted twice, then the motor died and it was safely in the dock.

Althea lived about five miles from the harbour. Her compact house was built on a low bluff overlooking a small sheltered bay. It was set back from the beach about a hundred yards. It was hard to see it clearly in the darkness, but as they drove off the main road and down the narrow driveway, Katherine could see that it was a typical beach cottage, all on one floor, with a low roof and surrounded by scrub pines.

As they stood on the covered porch and Luke rang the doorbell, Katherine began to suffer an attack of nerves. She looked at Luke.

'You're sure she won't mind?' she asked.

'Now, stop that,' he ordered sharply. 'Didn't I tell you it was all right? Besides, if she won't let you in you have my permission to sleep in the car.'

'Thanks a lot,' she said drily. She was about to retort that she should have known better than to let him talk her into anything when the porch light went on and the door opened.

Althea Dillon was a tall woman, much taller than Katherine, with a dark majestic beauty that was a feminine version of her brother. She had that same air of reserve, of restraint, and the same flashing dark eyes that spoke of banked fires beneath the calm exterior.

'Come in,' she said, and opened the door wider. Her voice was low and melodious. 'Did you have any trouble finding it in the dark?'

'No trouble,' said Luke. He stepped inside, propelling a hesitant Katherine before him. He shut the door and turned to his sister. 'You remember Katie, don't you, Althea?'

The tall woman glanced at Katherine, eyes widened a little in surprise, then dawning with recognition.

'Of course,' she said, holding out a hand. 'From Bainbridge. Katherine Evans.'

'It's Katherine Croft, now,' Luke remarked casually, setting down their suitcases. 'She is—or was—a married lady.'

Katherine grasped Althea's hand. The warmth of the welcoming pressure reassured her. 'It's nice to see you again, Althea,' she said. 'I hope this isn't a terrible imposition. Luke assured me it would be all right.'

'Of course,' said Althea, smiling. 'I've told him repeatedly to bring his friends up for the weekend.'

A quick glance passed between Althea and Luke, but it was gone before Katherine could read it. She assumed that it had some reference to Luke's other female guests and hoped Althea wasn't putting her in that category.

As they followed Althea into the main part of the house, she asked them if they had eaten. 'There's some cold roast beef and salad in the fridge.' Katherine told her they had stopped for a bite in Anacortes, and then stepped into the most delightful and unusual room she had ever seen.

It was enormous, with one whole wall given over to windows. The curtains were drawn and outside was a dark expanse of sea, with only a few distant blinking lights to remind her of civilisation. One corner of the room was dominated by a huge concert grand piano. There was music scattered on the bench and rack.

In another corner was a complicated recording and stereo system, with records and tapes on every available surface. On one wall was a massive stone fireplace, even larger and more impressive than the one in her old home on Bainbridge Island.

The floors were a dull creamy terrazzo with scatterings of Indian and Oriental rugs. In the middle of the room, grouped around the fireplace, were several large comfortable-looking chairs and a sofa, all upholstered in a dark hunter green.

Over the fireplace was hung a life-size portrait of a dark-haired woman in a Spanish costume, a form-hugging red dress, low-cut, slit to the knee. Her hair was piled high on her head with a gem-encrusted comb at the back. A red rose was between her teeth. Katherine stared up at it, fascinated.

She turned to Althea, 'Is that you?' she asked.

Althea laughed. 'No, I'm afraid I don't rate a portrait at this stage in my career. I have sung *Carmen*, however, at La Scala and Venice, although not yet as well as she did.' She looked up at the portrait with reverence. 'That's the great Risë Stevens, probably the finest singing actress of our time in her voice range.'

She turned to Katherine, the spell broken. 'Come, I'll show you to your room. Luke, will you carry the bags?' She looked at him again the same way she had earlier, a question in her dark eyes. Luke shook his head imperceptibly. Then she turned away and said, 'You can have your usual room.'

Katherine found her room enchanting. It was at the front of the house, with another expanse of windows on the sea that promised a fine view in the daylight. It was quite simple, even austere, with a single bed, a dresser and small mirrored dressing table.

'You and I will share a bathroom,' said Althea when Luke had gone. 'I detest having a man using my bathroom, so I insisted on two in the bedroom wing just in case.'

That night the three of them sat up late in the dimmed main room listening to music. Luke sat in the shadows, the flickering firelight playing over his fine features, his eyes half shut, his elbows resting on the arms of his chair, hands together with his fingertips under his chin. He had kept on the dark trousers of his business suit, but exchanged his dress shirt for a soft white knit that moulded his broad shoulders and strong chest.

In the firelight, Katherine, sitting across from him, glanced at him overtly from time to time. His shirt was open at the neck and she imagined the pulse beating at the hollow of his throat.

In the intervals between records, Althea and Luke spoke knowledgeably about the music, mostly opera. Katherine realised that she was seeing a side of Luke she never knew existed. It slowly dawned on her that this strong, reserved, cultivated man was no longer the passionate, awkward boy she had known. Neither was he the domineering and autocratic lawyer she saw in the office. In his comments about the music he displayed a sensitivity and appreciation for beauty that she found baffling and disturbing. This frightened her a little. She looked at him for the first time as if he were a stranger.

She listened to them as they discussed the merits of the two leading tenors of the day, both of whom Katherine, who loved opera, thought were fine singers. Both had appeared with the Seattle Opera, and Luke and Althea were discussing them from the point of view of musicianship. They were on opposite sides, and soon were arguing heatedly, although without animosity.

Althea stood in front of the slowly dying fire facing them. Katherine thought she looked every inch an opera star, with her mass of heavy dark hair piled on her head, her loose flowing velvet robe of deep cherry red, the expressive hands now raised in front of her to make a point.

'No, no, no, Luke!' she exclaimed, her deep voice vibrant with emotion. 'Pavarotti is simply the superior voice. He can do far more with his instrument than Domingo. He can sing anything.'

Luke had jumped to his feet and was pacing back and forth. 'I see your point, Althea,' he said, stopping beside her, 'but you're talking about technical perfection and I'm talking about tone quality. There's no comparison. Pavarotti sounds like a tin whistle compared to Domingo. It's like comparing a piccolo with a cello.'

Katherine could contain herself no longer. Both of them were more knowledgeable than she, but she trusted her own judgment.

'I wonder if you both aren't missing the real point,' she said quietly. 'They are both great artists and fine musicians. Domingo's voice is far more pleasing than Pavarotti's, but he doesn't have Pavarotti's technical perfection. I enjoy them both for what they do so well—better than anyone else. The real point is that they are both devoted to cultivating their own unique gifts.'

Althea and Luke stared at her for a few moments in stunned silence. Then Althea smiled, shrugging a little.

'It sounds as though you've given the matter a great deal of thought,' she said. 'I hate to admit it, but I think you're right.'

She turned to Luke, who stood with his hands in his trousers pockets frowning down at his feet. He glanced at Katherine, then at his sister.

'She has a mind of her own, if that's what you mean,' he muttered grudgingly. Then he gave Katherine a penetrating look. 'However, that doesn't necessarily mean she's always right.' He stretched long arms above his head, flexing his shoulder muscles and yawning. 'Now, if you don't mind, I'm going to bed.'

He turned on his heel and walked out of the

room. Althea stared after him, an enigmatic look of calm appraisal on her face, then she began to poke the dying embers of the fire.

'Luke looks tired,' she said, busy with the fire, not looking at Katherine.

Katherine had stood up, cheeks blazing, hands clenched at her side. She was stunned by Luke's rudeness and very sorry she had come. She decided to leave the next day.

'Yes,' she said evenly, 'he's been working very hard.' She wondered just how much Althea knew about the past, or that Luke and she were working together.

Althea had turned. She stood leaning one shoulder against the mantelpiece. 'Odd coincidence, wasn't it?' she asked. 'Luke happening to come on this case to the firm where you work.'

Katherine gave her a quick look. She did know. 'Yes,' she said, 'it was.'

'He tells me you're virtually indispensable to him—in a business way, of course.'

Katherine was surprised that he had discussed her at all with his sister. 'I'm glad he thinks so,' she said. 'Although I don't think he'd thank you for telling me.'

Anthea smiled. 'No, I guess not. I don't imagine he's the easiest person in the world to work for. Probably quite demanding—and not very free with his compliments.'

'Not to me, anyway,' Katherine said lightly. She started to leave. 'I'll say goodnight, Althea. Thank you for a pleasant evening. I enjoyed the music so much.'

Althea said goodnight, then watched Katherine as she walked away from her, deep in thought.

The next morning Katherine awoke very early. The unaccustomed absence of the traffic noises of the city and the chirping of birds coming through her open window disturbed her sleep.

She stretched lazily in her narrow bed. The sun was already up. She glanced at her watch. Seventhirty. There wasn't a sound in the house. Katherine knew that Luke had been dead tired last night, and thought that Althea, like most performers, was probably a late riser.

On an impulse she decided to go for an early swim before the others got up. She jumped out of bed, put on her cream coloured bikini and grabbed a towel from the bathroom. She pinned her long golden hair securely at the top of her head.

She found her way down to the beach with no trouble. It was quite close to the beach. The tide must be in, she thought. The beach was smooth and clean with hardly any rocks underfoot. Katherine laid her towel down on the fine sand, slipped off her sandals, and ran to the water's edge. She walked slowly into the surf.

The water was cold, and she shivered a little. It was a sparkling greenish colour, so clear that she could see the bottom. She drew in a deep breath and let her body sink into it. She swam out about a hundred yards, then began to feel so numb from the freezing water that she decided she'd better turn back before she got cramp.

Suddenly she felt strong hands grasp her shoulders and turn her around, and found herself gazing into Luke's furious dark eyes.

'What the hell do you think you're doing out here swimming all alone?' he barked at her. 'You know better than that!'

Her teeth were chattering with the cold by now, but anger began to rise up in her, warming her. 'Let go of me, you big bully!' she demanded furiously. 'I know what I'm doing.'

'Sure you do,' he sneered, loosening his grip and pushing her away. In spite of his tone, Katherine could sense something like relief in his voice, and she wondered fleetingly if he had thought she was in trouble and was worried about her. Then he grinned. 'Race you back,' he challenged.

'You're on,' she said. She turned and started swimming back as hard as she could.

She kept ahead of him until they were about twenty yards from the shore, then he darted forward with a tremendous surge of splashing water which cascaded over her, almost swamping her.

He was there standing on the beach, ready with one arm extended, when she arrived, panting and spluttering.

'You rat!' she cried as she grasped the strong hand and allowed him to pull her out. 'I should have known you'd do that. You never did race fair!'

She shook herself free, glaring at him. He was grinning, a self-satisfied smirk on his face, legs apart, hands on his hips. Then she started to giggle. Luke threw back his head and roared. They stood there for a moment, dripping and laughing, and Katherine was transported back to her girlhood.

The next thing she knew, Luke had stopped laughing. He was looking at her now, a long hungry look, a conquering, determined look. Then, making a gruff little sound in the back of his throat, he moved the step towards her that separated them, and she found herself enfolded in those powerful slippery arms.

He held her so tightly she could barely breathe. Instinctively, her arms went around his neck and she lifted her face to his. With another groan, 'Katie,' he breathed, his mouth was on hers. She tasted the salt still on his lips as her own mouth opened to receive him.

In his arms, their bodies pressed together longingly, Katherine felt a sense of rightness, of fitness, as if she had always belonged there, as if the two of them had been together since the beginning of time.

She had stopped shivering and could feel his heart steadily pounding against hers, the skin of his bare chest warm against her breasts. It was more than a physical response, even though the feel of his hardening body pressed against hers made her blood tingle.

He dropped to his knees in the sand, pulling her down so that he could bury his dark head in the deep cleavage of her bathing suit. She could feel the warmth of his hot mouth, as it moved over the fullness of breast exposed by the brief top.

As she wound her hands through the crisp dark hair, drying now in the sun, it dawned on her in a sudden burst of absolute certainty that she loved this man with all her heart and soul. But with this realization came a cold shaft of fear. Her hands stopped their loving stroking and her blood turned cold. She knew she was in terrible and imminent danger. Luke would never forgive her for what she had done to him. He wanted her physically, that was quite obvious, but it wasn't in him to trust anyone, much less someone who had already betrayed him once, wounded that proud male ego. And without trust there could be no love.

He would need to humiliate her, to wreak his revenge on her, over and over again. To love this man, to respond to him, would mean the death of her soul. With a little cry she broke out of his arms. Without a backward glance she ran up the path and into the house.

CHAPTER SEVEN

BACK in her room, calmer now, Katherine was surprised to see that it was only eight o'clock. She had only been on the beach for half an hour. It had seemed like an eternity. She stripped off her bikini and got in the shower. There wasn't a sound from Althea's bedroom.

As she showered and dried herself, she tried to push aside the insistent reminder of her feelings for Luke, but without success. In his arms she had felt alive again, a whole woman instead of a pale shadow of one. Under his touch the tight bud of her loneliness had opened and flowered. Standing now in the bathroom, the damp towel clutched to her, she ached for him.

But she couldn't dismiss the thought of the way he had treated her that first night at her house, the hatred and contempt in his eyes as he had rejected her so brutally. Never could she risk that happening again.

She put on her light blue robe and sat by the window staring blindly out at the deserted beach. Every time the thought of Luke pierced her heart and set her pulses racing, she tried to imagine some small detail of her pleasant life before Luke had re-entered it. Her comfortable little house, her rose garden, her interesting job, her easy relationship with Jim Hawkins.

It all felt flat, tasteless, lifeless. But safe, she thought, setting her jaw with determination. She knew what she had to do. She dressed hurriedly in the white sharkskin pants and striped shirt she had worn last night on the trip up, pinned her hair back severely and went out to the kitchen.

The fresh aroma of coffee greeted her. Luke was standing at the kitchen range, his back towards her. He was still in his dark swimming trunks, but had slipped the white knit shirt on. Katherine drew in her breath sharply at the sight of his tall masculine form. Just to be in the same room with him took her breath away.

He uttered an oath and started to shake the pan on the stove. Then, out of the corner of his eye, he caught sight of her and made a face.

'How in the hell do you make coffee?' he muttered.

She went to his side and looked down at the foul mess he was brewing in a saucepan. She sighed.

'Not like that,' she said. She rummaged in the cupboard, found an electric percolator and proceeded to make a fresh pot.

Luke stood by silently watching her. Finally, he said, 'I was going to bring you a cup. An apology.' She looked up at him swiftly. His expression was contrite. 'I promised you I wouldn't touch you, and then it's the first thing I do.'

Katherine looked away. 'It doesn't matter. I think I'd better get back to town today anyway.'

'Why?' he asked quickly.

'Oh, I just have things to do,' she replied vaguely.

'I said I was sorry,' he muttered. 'I don't know what more you want.'

She could sense him standing close beside her, feel his breath on her cheek. She though of the times he and Selma had left the office together, of the reputation that had preceded him to the office. She knew she was jealous, and she hated the feeling.

She looked up at him. 'Look,' she said curtly, 'I'm going back to Seattle. If you'll take me down to Orcas I'll catch the ferry to Anacortes and get on a bus.'

'You're chicken,' he jeered. 'What's the matter? Afraid of ruffling that placid phoney exterior, that safe little artificial life you've built up for yourself?'

'Not at all,' she replied calmly, her heart pounding underneath. She handed him a mug of coffee. 'Anyway, it's no concern of yours.'

At that moment Althea came into the kitchen. She had on a floor-length white terrycloth robe.

'Oh, I'm glad you made some coffee,' she said. She glanced at the pan on the stove and made a face. 'I see Luke's been practising his culinary arts again!'

'Althea,' Katherine said hurriedly, 'I've really got to get back to Seattle today. If Luke will drive me to Orcas . . .'

'Oh, for God's sake, shut up about that, will you?' Luke snapped angrily. 'I should get back to town myself anyway.'

He stalked out of the room. The two women stood looking after him, then glanced uneasily at each other. Althea cocked her head thoughtfully, Then she smiled.

'You seem to have penetrated a few defences there,' she remarked lightly.

'Oh, I doubt that,' Katherine replied. 'He has the hide of an elephant.' And the memory of one, too, she added to herself. Then she coloured as she remembered that that wasn't always true, that once in his life, at least, he had made himself vulnerable to her.

Althea busied herself pouring juice out of a container from the refrigerator. 'Do you find Luke much changed after so long?' she asked.

Katherine didn't want to think of Luke at all, but she did, just to be polite. 'In some ways he's exactly the same,' she said slowly. 'He always was sure of what he wanted and how to get it. But he's much more polished now.'

'You cared for him a great deal, didn't you?' said Althea softly.

'Yes. Yes, of course I did. When we were children.'

'Yet you married Brian Croft.' The low voice was kind, but insistent.

Katherine sipped her coffee nervously. 'That was a misunderstanding all the way around,' she said finally.

Althea raised one eyebrow, just as Luke had. 'You didn't love Brian?' she asked.

Katherine rinsed out her coffee mug and set it in the sink. Then she turned to the other woman. 'Althea, I know you mean well. But there's no point in raking up the past. Luke will be leaving as soon as the case is over, and the whole thing will be forgotten. My marriage to Brian Croft wasn't a marriage in any sense of the word.'

'Does Luke know that?'

'Luke couldn't care less,' Katherine said flatly. Then she forced a smile. 'I'd better get my things together. Thank you for being so kind—and welcoming.'

The drive home was a silent one. Luke sat behind the wheel deep in thought, his eyes on the road. Katherine stared miserably out of the window, her head pounding, every muscle in her body tense. It was raining by the time they reached Katherine's house, a slow Seattle drizzle.

Luke switched off the engine and turned to face her. She reached to open the door, trying to avoid his eyes without being too obvious.

'Thanks for the lift, Luke. I'm sorry to make you leave early. I hope I haven't spoiled your weekend.' Her tone was polite and formal.

He waved a hand. 'No problem. I wanted to get some work done in the office anyway.'

Her eyes widened. 'You're going to the office?'

'Sure,' he said. 'Why not? Selma's down there working on answers to first wave interrogatories. I want to see how she's doing.'

'I see,' Katherine said evenly. She opened the door and got out. 'I'll see you on Monday,' she said. She slammed the door shut and started to walk up the path to her house. She heard him start the engine and drive off. At the door to the house she turned just in time to see the car disappear around the corner, then she unlocked the door and went inside.

As she unpacked and put her things away in the quiet of her own house, Katherine's spirits revived a little. By late afternoon the throbbing in her head began to subside. She poured herself a glass of sherry before dinner and went out to sit on her tiny patio near the rose garden, drinking in the fragrance. The rain had stopped and a pale sun cast shadows through the graceful vine maples at the side of the garden.

She found herself wondering what Luke and Selma were doing. Were they alone in the office? Would Luke take her out to dinner? Had he ever taken her to Althea's house on the island? Did he hold Selma in his arms the way he had held her? Kiss her with the same hunger?

Katherine hugged herself tightly and shut her eyes against the tormenting visions of her imagination. It didn't matter, she told herself. I forgot him once and I can forget him again. If there was one certainty in her life, it was that there was no future for her with Luke Dillon.

It rained all day Sunday and it was still raining on Monday morning. Everyone in the office was complaining about the ruined weekend. Jim Hawkins was back from Cincinnati. He had left a small package on Katherine's desk, and appeared around the corner, grinning broadly, just as she was opening it.

It was an exquisite paperweight, with a red velvet-covered base and a heavy-domed crystal top. Inside the crystal was a setting of sparkling stones in the shape of a red rose. She looked up at him with delight.

'Jim, it's beautiful!' she said. She placed it on top of the papers in the wooden tray on her desk. 'I love it. Thank you so much.'

'Glad you like it,' he said, pleased. 'I noticed your old snowstorm was missing and guessed you'd either lost it, or broken it, or gotten tired of it. In any event, it's my pleasure.'

He gave her a little salute and went into Luke's office. In a few minutes Luke came out, looking harried.

'I can't find the defendants' first request for production,' he barked at her.

'It's on your desk,' she said calmly, envisioning the mountain of paper there.

'That's the *second* request,' he snarled. 'I want the first one. F-I-R-S-T,' spelled, glaring at her.

'That's there, too,' she said with infinite patience. 'Would you like me to find it for you?'

He growled out a negative, started back to his office, then abruptly turned on his heel. 'Did you find Selma's draft interrogatory answers on your desk?'

'I haven't looked yet. I just got in.'

He was back at her desk now, waiting impatiently, fingers drumming on the top of it. As she started searching for the document, he picked up the paperweight and examined it.

'This is new,' he stated. 'A present?'

She coloured. 'Yes, it is. Put it down—you'll break it.'

'What happened to the old one you used to have on your desk? The snowstorm?'

She gave him a sharp look. Their eyes met briefly before she looked away. 'I lost it,' she lied.

'I see,' he said, his mouth set in a hard line. 'Just got tired of it, is that it? Off with the old and on with the new? Quite a habit with you.'

She thrust papers at him. 'Here,' she said, 'here are the answers you wanted.' She was determined not to let him get a rise out of her.

He handed the papers back. 'These are to be typed up. Today. They're due Thursday.'

Katherine took the papers from him and he walked off. She sat down at her desk, her head swimming so that she could hardly see the typewriter keys. He had obviously noticed the snowstorm paperweight he had given her before she'd had a chance to put it away. And he had remembered it.

For the next two days Luke was gone from the office, in San Francisco at settlement meetings with the defendants. Jim was back in Cincinnati inspecting documents, and Katherine spent each day glued to her desk, typing the interrogatory answers.

Selma was in charge of preparing the answers, and by Wednesday afternoon Katherine could cheerfully have cut her throat. She had come grudgingly to admire the tall redhead's intelligence and legal ability, but without Luke or Jim there to guide her, she was obviously unsure of herself and kept changing things so that Katherine had retyped several pages half a dozen times.

Finally, by five o'clock, Katherine had finished the last answer and had just typed the signature page. She sighed with relief as she collated the pages carefully to make sure they were numbered properly and glanced hurriedly over them for typos.

She said goodnight to Teresa, who was racing past her towards the elevator, and took the document into Selma's office.

'I think that's it, Selma,' she said. 'Ready for signature. You can look it over and sign it. I'll have the copies made and serve it myself tomorrow.'

Selma was sitting behind her desk. The top of it was covered with documents, notebooks and thick volumes from the law library. She looked at the tidy stack of freshly typed pages and then up at Katherine. She wore fashionably large tinted glasses with heavy pale green frames. Her red hair flowed loosely to her shoulders. She stared at Katherine for a long time.

'Thanks a lot,' she said at last. 'I know you must be sick of it.'

Katherine laughed. 'Well, it's no longer my favourite reading material!' She flexed her hands. 'My fingers feel as though they're about to fall off.' She turned to go. 'See you tomorrow.'

She heard Selma's voice calling her. 'Yes?' she said, turning back, her hand on the doorknob.

Selma hesitated, watching her carefully with cool, appraising green eyes. The heavy gold bracelets on her arm jangled as she raised her hand to take off the glasses.

'I didn't realise you and Luke Dillon were old friends,' she said. Her voice was high-pitched and aggressive.

Katherine's eyes widened. 'What makes you think we were?' she asked.

Selma stood up, skirted around her desk and walked toward her with purposeful strides.

'Does it matter?' she drawled. She sat on the edge of her desk, her palms flat on its surface, her head cocked to one side. 'Actually, he just mentioned that he'd had lunch with your brother one day last week.' She snorted. 'I didn't even know you had a brother.'

Katherine was surprised. Luke and Neal having lunch together again? On the other hand, why not? They were old friends.

She said nothing. She didn't owe Selma Boyd-Richards an explanation of her past or her present life.

'I was just wondering,' Selma went on, her eyes narrowing, 'just where matters stood between you now.'

Katherine opened her eyes wide. 'What in the world difference does that make to you?' she asked finally. 'You're married.'

Selma waved a hand in the air, dimissing her marriage. 'Oh, that. Dirk and I have a sensible marriage,' she explained patiently, as if to a child. Her tone was self-satisfied and complacent. 'We're best friends. We don't believe in bonds and shackles.'

Katherine was curious. 'But what about your children?'

Selma stared at her, aghast. 'Children? What children? No, thank you. I didn't go to school for seven years and claw my way into the best law firm in Seattle to tie myself down with a bunch of snotty-nosed kids!'

Katherine was silent, remembering how when she had married Brian, knowing she didn't love him, she had consoled herself with the thought of at least having children to care for. It was only when she realised that it would never happen that she had given up on the marriage.

She looked at Selma with pity and said quietly, 'You have nothing to fear from me. Luke and I knew each other as children, That's all. There is no relationship except what you see in the office.' Not quite true, she amended to herself, but she intended that it would be from now on. 'Besides,' she added, 'he's not my type.'

Selma eyed her coolly. 'No,' she agreed, 'I don't imagine he would be.'

Katherine went back to her desk. She felt so tired. The office was deserted. She heard Selma leave as she was gathering her things together. As she started down the hall to the elevator, she heard her telephone ring.

She hesitated, debating whether or not to go back and answer it. Her aching body told her to forget it, but her sense of duty won out.

'Hello,' she said.

'It's me,' came a familiar voice. Luke! Her heart turned over. 'I want to dictate something. Got a pad and pencil handy?'

'Where in the world are you?' she asked.

'In Portland.'

'What are you doing in Portland?'

'We had engine trouble and had to put down. I've only got half an hour. Ready?'

By the time she found a pencil and pad he had already started dictating. It was the terms of a settlement agreement with one of the defendants. He clipped out the words in his usual precise, positive way, every detail well worked out in his mind.

'Okay, that's it,' he said finally. 'Type it up and leave it on my desk. I want it for the meeting tomorrow morning.'

Katherine sighed wearily. 'Listen, Luke,' she began to explain, 'I've had a hard day. I'm so tired, I'm numb. I don't think I could type another stroke.'

'But I need that first thing in the morning!' he bellowed.

Katherine began to get angry. 'Don't yell at me like that!' she shouted at him. 'What do you think I am, a machine you can just turn on and off? I'm a human being! I am not—repeat, *not*—going to stay here and type this thing tonight, even if it means losing the case!'

She was trembling, her pulse racing, more angry than she could ever remember being in her life. She breathed heavily into the telephone.

There was a short silence. Then he spoke, his voice softer, less demanding. 'Okay, okay, calm down. I'm sorry. But, damn it, I need that typed tonight.' He thought a moment. 'Have you got a typewriter at home?'

'Yes, I have,' she said, hissing the words.

'Tell you what. You go on home now, have a nice relaxing bath, a drink, some dinner, and then type it up at home. Would you do that for me? Please?'

She began to thaw under the unaccustomed humility and courtesy in his tone. 'Well . . .' she began.

'That's a good girl! Listen, they're announcing my flight. Thanks a million.' The phone clicked in her ear.

Sighing wearily, Katherine hung up the phone and stood looking down at it for a full minute. She sighed. 'That man!' she said aloud.

She hated to admit it, but Luke was right. She soaked in the tub for half an hour, until the water got cold. Then, brushing out her hair until it fell in gleaming folds to her shoulders, she felt like a human being again. She put on her light blue robe, tied the sash and went into the kitchen.

There she poured herself a glass of wine and ate some cheese and crackers, an apple, and put on the coffee. She was still tired, but the frazzled harried feeling was gone.

She got out her portable typewriter, set it on the kitchen table and sat down to type out the dictation she had taken over the telephone.

In spite of a lingering anger at his demanding attitude, as she typed Katherine was once again impressed with the conciseness of Luke's thought and his clear manner of expression. It was a short document, only two typewritten pages, clear and to the point. It only took her about half an hour to do. She probably should have stayed and done it at the office, she thought as she put the typewriter away, but at that time she had been in no mood to face it. She'd take it in with her in the morning so he'd have it for his meeting.

She poured herself a cup of coffee and was debating whether or not to scramble a couple of eggs when the doorbell rang.

Living alone, Katherine was wary about unexpected night visitors, and she walked quietly into the darkened living room to check that she had fastened the chain bolt on the door. She was relieved to see that she had.

'Who is it?' she called.

'It's me, Luke.'

'Oh, for heaven's sake,' she muttered as she unlatched the door and pulled it open.

It was raining gently, but the air was warm. He stood there facing her, in the glow of the porch light. His hair sparkled with raindrops and his shoulders were hunched. The collar of his light raincoat was turned up to protect the back of his neck.

'What in the world are you doing here?' she asked. She clutched the front of her robe tightly.

'I'm taking a shower at the moment,' he said dryly. 'Can I come in?'

She stepped back and opened the door. 'You're all wet,' she remarked.

'I know,' he agreed, taking off his coat and running a hand over his wet head.

'I'll get you a towel,' she offered.

'No, thanks.' He sniffed the air. 'But I could use a cup of coffee.'

Katherine took his coat and hung it up to dry. 'Are you hungry?' she asked over her shoulder.

'Starved. I came straight from the airport. Did you get it typed?'

They were in the kitchen. She pointed at the table. 'There it is.'

Luke sat down and began to read, giving the typed pages every bit of his attention, in total concentration. Katherine, trying not to think of what it did to her to have him sitting there, so close, busied herself at the kitchen counter.

'Did it seem to you there's a chance for settlement?' she asked as she took butter and eggs from the refrigerator.

'Yes,' he murmured absently. 'But you know how those things go. I think they know we've got a damn good case, though, and aren't afraid to pursue it to the bitter end.'

Katherine got out the frying pan. 'If we settle, you'll be going back to New York.' It was more a question than a statement.

She could feel his eyes on her as she stirred the eggs.

'I'm not sure,' he said at last.

She turned to face him, eyes wide, hand poised in mid-air over the bowl of eggs. 'What do you mean?'

'I'm thinking seriously about buying my old home on Bainbridge,' he said, watching her from under hooded eyelids.

'But your work,' she said in confusion. 'What about your firm in New York?' Oh, Lord, she prayed, don't let him stay here. She knew she could give him up if she never saw him again, but if he stayed in town—that might be a different story.

He shrugged. 'Your firm has offered me a partnership.'

'I see,' she said in a small voice. She turned back to her cooking.

'You don't sound overjoyed at the prospect,' he remarked dryly.

'What you do is none of my business,' she answered tartly.

She scrambled the eggs and made toast for the two of them, poured him a cup of coffee and put the plate in front of him.

'Eat it while it's hot,' she said.

'This is fine,' he said, putting the pages down. He ate hungrily. They were both silent.

'That was very good,' he said when he had finished. 'I get tired of restaurant food.' He looked at her. 'I didn't know you could cook.'

'Scrambled eggs are not exactly French cuisine,' Katherine remarked as she got up to clear the table.

She could sense his eyes following her as she carried the dishes to the sink and rinsed them out.

'I called Selma from the airport,' he said casually. He lit a cigarette.

'Oh?' Katherine put the butter in the refrigerator.

'She just happend to mention an interesting conversation you and she had this afternoon.'

Katherine came back to the table with the coffee pot, wondering what in the world Selma could have told him that he found so interesting. She looked at him. His eyes were narrowed, his mouth set in an angry line. He held up his cup and she poured the coffee.

He took a sip. 'Of course,' he said, his lip curling, 'I guess I already knew I wasn't your type.'

She poured herself a cup of coffee, aware of his eyes tracing her every movement. She set the pot down on the table and sat in her chair opposite him.

She sighed. 'Selma had no right to repeat that. But since she did, I'd better tell you that she was, in a sense, warning me off you. I just wanted to assure her that there was no tie between us.'

'I'm not Selma's property,' said Luke in an even tone.

'She seems to think you're fair game, at any rate,' Katherine replied. Then she added with a wry smile, 'And I haven't noticed that you've found her actually repulsive.' She looked at him over her coffee cup.

'Oh, that,' he shrugged, dismissing Selma. 'She's good company.' Katherine wondered just how far good company went. They were silent for a moment. Then, suddenly, he asked, 'Are you going to marry Jim Hawkins?'

She gave him a quick look. 'No,' she said finally. She set down her coffee cup and looked at him again. 'I'm not going to marry anybody.'

'You're not still married to Brian?'

'No.'

'Divorced?'

'Yes,' she said dully. 'I filed about a month after the wedding.'

Luke's eyes widened. He thought for a moment,

then reached across the table and put his hand over hers.

'What happened, Katie?' he asked softly.

She turned her head away. 'Luke,' she said hoarsely. 'let's change the subject.'

He said nothing for a while, just sat staring at her, his hand still resting lightly on hers.

'You know,' he said at last, 'you're more beautiful now than ever. You shouldn't waste all that loveliness shut up here alone.'

She gave him a defiant look. 'I'm perfectly content with my life,' she said. She pulled her hand away and stood up. 'It's getting late, Luke.'

In a second, he was out of his chair and standing before her. He put his hands on her shoulders and gave her a searching look. She clutched the front of her robe tightly shut.

He gave her a little shake, his dark eyes brooding, flashing fire. 'Why in the hell did you throw me over?' he muttered. 'Why did you have to do such a terrible, destructive thing? We were made for each other, like one person.'

'Oh, Luke,' Katherine sighed wearily, 'don't! Please don't. I can't stand any more raking over the past.' She turned her head away, determined to resist him.

He put a hand on her loose, flowing hair and pulled her roughly to him. His hard mouth was on hers, demanding, forceful. She felt her knees go weak. She summoned up all her strength and twisted her mouth away from his, pushing at his chest with clenched fists.

'No, no, no,' she cried. 'Don't! Please. Will you

please just leave me alone?' She turned angry eyes on him. 'Haven't I paid enough? Aren't you satisfied?'

Luke smiled wickedly, dropped his eyes lazily to rest on her heaving breast. In the struggle her robe had come loose and the full curves underneath were half-revealed by the gap in the closing. He raised his eyes to hers. Her cheeks were flaming.

'Satisfied?' he drawled. 'No, Katie, I won't be satisfied until I have all of you. And I will—make no mistake about that.'

She looked away, felt him withdraw, and heard him leave the room. The front door slammed behind him. Slowly she walked into the living room. She reached up and fastened the chain bolt on the door.

She felt like a trapped animal. She admitted to herself that she loved him, that she had always loved him, from the time they were children together. She began to wonder if she shouldn't just give herself to him and get it over with. That would satisfy him, slake his demonic thirst for revenge, and then he might leave her alone.

She went into the bathroom and looked at herself in the mirror. Her robe was dishevelled, her hair tangled where he had grabbed it. She gazed at the unnaturally bright hazel eyes, the high colour on her cheeks.

Why not? she asked herself again. His touch was like fire, his kiss still burning on her bruised mouth. She brush the back of one hand against her lips and shuddered. Why not?

But she knew she couldn't do it. She was emotionally and physically exhausted, her defences at their weakest. Tomorrow it would all look different. She hadn't struggled so painfully to make a decent peaceful life for herself just to throw it all away now to satisfy Luke Dillon's male pride.

She would fight him, she decided, as she slipped wearily into bed, with every ounce of her mind and will.

CHAPTER EIGHT

For the next two weeks the pressure of work on the paper case slackened as the settlement negotiations slowly proceeded. This was always a delicate matter, each side determined to get the most for his client and make the least concessions.

With the easing of the frantic rush to get documents prepared and deadlines met, Katherine had a chance to put the files in order and to give some attention to Jim's other cases. The filing had piled up in her basket for so long she was afraid she'd never find anything.

After that night at her house, when Luke had issued his threat to have her on his terms, his whole attitude towards her at work had changed. This was partly due, she knew, to the more relaxed pace, but he made it clear in unmistakable ways exactly what was on his mind.

He would sit on the edge of her desk whenever he had to speak to her, leaning across so that their heads were close together, those brooding dark eyes boring into hers. She could sense his gaze following her whenever she walked down the hall in front of him. He would manage to touch her arm or brush up against her at every opportunity.

True to her own determination to keep up her defences at all costs, she treated him with unfailing courtesy and a remote coolness that was her customary role in the office anyway. She hoped the others didn't notice what he was doing, but that hope was doomed to disappointment and shattered beyond repair when one day in the coffee room Teresa drew her aside.

'That man is eating you alive with his eyes,' she whispered.

They were sitting at one of the round tables on their afternoon coffee break. It was late, and only one other table at the far end of the room was occupied.

'What man?' Katherine asked innocently.

Teresa snorted. 'What man? Who are you trying to kid? If a man like Luke Dillon looked at me the way he does you, believe me, I'd know it!' She giggled. 'Doesn't it make you feel naked?'

'Oh, Teresa, honestly,' Katherine exploded. 'What an imagination! Is that all you ever think about?'

'There's something else?' Teresa asked in mock wonderment.

Katherine got up from the table. 'Well, believe me, nothing about Luke Dillon interests me, so will you please stop talking about it?'

As she turned to go she found herself staring into the hostile green eyes of Selma Boyd-Richards. She averted her gaze and, head held high, walked past her to the sink. She rinsed out her coffee cup and started back to her desk.

Teresa caught up with her and fell into step beside her. 'Did you see the look she gave you?' she breathed excitedly. 'If looks could kill you'd be dead and buried!'

'Apparently Selma's imagination is as active as yours,' Katherine replied tartly.

Luke appeared at the door to his office as Katherine and Teresa passed by. Katherine saw his eyes travel from the top of her head down to her toes and back up to meet her eyes. She set her face in a polite mask and started to walk past him, but he caught her arm.

'Come into my office,' he said, his tone insinuating.

'Yes, Mr Dillon,' she said sweetly, freeing herself unobtrusively from his grasp. 'Shall I get my notebook?'

'That won't be necessary.' There was an edge of impatience in his voice. She followed him inside. 'Shut the door,' he said. She obeyed, then stood quietly before him, hands clasped in front of her.

Luke paced over to the window and stared down at the busy street below, as if collecting his thoughts. Then he came back to the front of his desk and leaned against it, his arms crossed in front of him, glaring at her.

'You've been avoiding me,' he snapped curtly. 'Why?'

'That's rather difficult to do, since we work together every day,' she said, sidestepping the issue.

He straightened up and took a step towards her. 'You know what I mean.'

'I'm afraid I don't,' she insisted, still polite and cool. 'Are you dissatisfied with my work, Mr Dillon? If so, I'm sure I could arrange for a suitable replacement.'

His brow was like thunder. He opened his mouth, made a gesture toward her, then narrowed his eyes. 'Okay,' he said, leaning back against the desk again, 'have it your way. For now. But you'll come around. You'll have to.'

'I doubt that very much,' she said, then turned to go. 'Is that all?'

He nodded curtly and she walked to the door. Then she heard him speak her name. 'Katie.' She turned. 'Don't be too sure of yourself. I can recall at least three quite recent occasions when the ice melted and you responded to me rather warmly. The thaw will set in again.'

'Don't bet on it,' she snapped, and walked out.

Jim Hawkins was standing at her desk when she emerged from Luke's office. During the settlement negotiations all depositions and document inspection had been called off, so that he was able to stay in Seattle and catch up on his other cases. He gave her an enquiring look.

'Trouble with the slave-driver?' he asked casually, and nodded towards Luke's office.

'Not really. I can handle him. Besides, if the case settles he'll be leaving soon.'

'And you'll be glad?' he asked, watching her closely.

'Absolutely delighted,' Katherine said fervently, and meant it.

He laughed. 'I've got tickets to the opera Wednesday night. Opening night of the season—*Il Trovatore*. Interested?'

'Oh, Jim, how lovely! Of course I'm interested.'

'We can have dinner downtown first, if you like.

That'll give us plenty of time to get to the Opera House by eight.'

'Sounds perfect,' she said.

For the next two days Luke and Jim were both tied up in meetings and Katherine had plenty of time to catch up on her filing. She also managed to leave the office promptly at five, take her whole lunch hour each day and full coffee breaks. With the pressure of the case relaxed she was sleeping better. Not having to face Luke every day and dodge his meaningful looks and innuendoes was a relief, too.

The night of the opera she and Jim had a leisurely dinner at a waterfront salmon house. They had a table by the window. Katherine loved looking out at the busy harbour, dark now by six o'clock, the blackish water dotted with blinking lights.

She enjoyed being with Jim. He made her feel comfortable and desirable without forcing himself on her. She knew he wasn't particularly fond of opera and had only got the tickets to please her.

'Jim,' she said over drinks, 'I really appreciate your taking me to the opera. Tell you what, I'll take you to a football game at the Kingdome. 'You'll have to tell me when the Mariners are playing however.'

He laughed. 'Seahawks, Katherine. The Mariners are the baseball team.' Her hand was resting on the white tablecloth and he covered it lightly with his own. 'You don't have to do that,' he said in a more serious tone. 'It's pleasure enough for me just to be with you. You're looking especially beautiful tonight.'

She had worn her black velveteen suit to work that day, exchanging the silk shirt for a scooped-necked white brocade with black beading in the coffee room after work. She had put on teardrop pearl earrings and greyish eyeshadow, and had piled her hair into a looser, fuller chignon at the top of her head.

'Thank you kindly, sir,' she said.

'You look—hmm—' he said thoughtfully, chin in hand, 'very regal. Like some Scandinavian queen.'

'My,' she said playfully, raising an eyebrow, 'you overwhelm me!'

He sighed. 'I only wish I did. Maybe I should take a lesson or two from Luke Dillon.'

Katherine stiffened and frowned. 'What do you mean?'

'I've seen the way he looks at you,' said Jim with a little grin.

'I have absolutely no interest in Luke Dillon,' she said firmly.

'He's a very determined guy.'

'He can determine away all he wants,' she said. 'for all the good it'll do him.'

'Well, I'm glad to hear it, but I doubt if it necessarily follows that it means you're going to fall into my waiting arms.' He glanced at her hopefully.

'Jim,' she said softly, turning her hand round in his to grasp it gently, 'I'm very fond of you.'

'But . . .' he added ruefully. 'Okay, I won't push. So long as you're not involved with anyone else. I can be patient.'

Their dinner was served then, and the conversation turned to more impersonal subjects. Watching him as they chatted companionably, Katherine wished she could love this decent man who obviously cared so much about her. He would never hurt her, never make unreasonable demands on her, would provide her with a secure comfortable life.

She was sorely tempted, but when he took her home that night, turned to her and put his arms around her, she knew it would never work. His lips were soft and undemanding, his touch gentle, and there was not the slightest spark of response in her. She knew he'd have her on any terms, but it wouldn't be fair to him to marry him without either love or desire.

The next day, just as she was finishing breakfast, the telephone rang. She set down her coffee cup and ran to the phone in the living room.

'Hello.'

'Katie? It's Neal,' came her brother's voice. He always sounded impatient and rushed over the phone, but today there was an extra edge of anxiety in his voice.

Katherine tensed. Why in the world was Neal calling her at eight o'clock in the morning?

'Yes, Neal. What's wrong?'

'Barbara's pregnant,' he said.

'Why, Neal,' she said in bewilderment, 'that's wonderful.' She knew they had desperately wanted another child for years. After Barbara's second miscarriage she thought they had given up hope.

Still, she didn't see what the emergency was.

'Well, it is and it isn't,' he said. He sounded distracted. 'I mean we're pleased, of course, but Barbara's had a hell of a time.'

'What can I do?' she asked quickly.

'God, Katie, I'm half out of my mind! I've *got* to go down to Buenos Aires for a week on a really critical business trip. I'll explain it later, but believe me, I've got to go.' She could hear him suck in his breath. 'But I can't leave Barbara. The doctor says she'll be okay if she stays in bed for the next few weeks, get her over the critical period. I've got a lot of vacation time coming and was planning to stay here as long as she needed me, but then this blasted trip came up.'

Katherine's mind raced. With the settlement negotiations going ahead on the paper case there was no reason why she couldn't take a week off work. She'd finished all her other filing, so that Jim would be able to put his hands on anything he needed.

'Katie!' came Neal's shout. 'Are you still there?'

'Yes, Neal, I'm here,' she soothed. 'When do you have to leave?'

'Today!' he barked. 'My plane leaves at four o'clock. Hell, I think I'll just quit the damn job! I can't ask you . . .'

'Neal,' Katherine interrupted, 'just be quiet for a minute and let me think.' But she had already made up her mind. 'I'll call Jim and let him know, then sort out a few things here.' She should stop the paper, she calculated mentally, and leave a note for the milkman. 'If your plane leaves at four you'll want to leave for the airport by two. I think I can make the twelve o'clock ferry.'

'God, Sis, you're a lifesaver! I knew I could count on you. I'll meet you on this side.'

'Neal,' she called before he could hang up.

'What about Nancy?' If she had to nurse Barbara she was worried that she wouldn't be able to look after the little girl at the same time.

'Oh, I'm taking Nancy with me. That's really the only reason I agreed to go.'

'Okay. See you soon. And, Neal, don't worry. It'll be all right.'

They hung up. Katherine began planning her schedule. Call the office first, she decided, and dialled.

'Powell, Cable and Hawkins,' came Sharon's cheerful voice. 'Good morning.'

'Hi, Sharon—it's Katherine. Is Jim in yet?'

'Just a minute, I'll ring.' Katherine heard the inter office phone buzz four times, then Sharon's voice came back on the line. 'I guess not,' she said. 'I haven't seen him yet.'

'Would you ask him to call me at home when he gets in?'

'Are you sick?'

'No. A family emergency has come up, though, and I have to be gone for a week. Tell him that. He can call me at my brother's on Bainbridge Island if he needs me.' She gave Sharon the number. 'I'll be home until ten o'clock, though, if he comes in by then.'

After she had hung up Katherine wrote notes to the paper boy and milkman and went into her bedroom to pack. She wouldn't need much, she decided, just a couple of changes and clean underwear. It was too cold to swim.

She straightened the house as best she could in the time she had, throwing out leftovers from the refrigerator and putting bread in the freezer.

By nine-thirty she was almost through. The telephone rang as she was packing her cosmetics and toilet articles. Jim, she thought, running to the phone.

'Hello.'

'Sharon tells me you're not coming in today,' barked an all too familiar voice.

Katherine felt her knees weaken and her heart started to pound. I *wish* he didn't have that effect on me, she said to herself.

'Hello, Luke,' she managed to say coolly. 'That's right. I'll be gone probably until next Wednesday or Thursday.'

'Well, you can't go,' he stated flatly. 'I need you here.'

She began to grow angry. Who did he think he was? 'No, you don't, Luke,' she said evenly. 'Everything is in order.'

'Damn it,' he shouted, 'I need some typing done! Now get down here right away. What makes you think you can take time off in the middle of an important case?'

Katherine struggled to remain calm. 'Neal's wife is sick and he has to go out of town. They need me. I'm going, and that's flat. Teresa is an excellent typist, and your work is always quite clear. You don't need me; Neal and Barbara do.'

There was silence at the other end. Then, 'What if Teresa can't do it?'

Katherine was exasperated, but half amused. The big baby! 'Then get Selma to do it. You seem to depend on her for everything else. Goodbye, Luke.'

She replaced the receiver, finished her packing and locked the door behind her.

Katherine had never seen her brother look so distraught. For all his gruff impatient ways, she knew he adored Barbara with the single-minded devotion only strong, self-willed men can feel.

'I don't think I should go at all,' he muttered as they sped away from the harbour towards the house.

'Don't be silly, Neal,' she said, trying to sound unconcerned. 'There's nothing you could do that I can't. Just fill me in on the details.' She glanced at him and her heart went out to him. His face was drawn and haggard, his colour ashen. She put a hand on his arm. 'I'm really quite capable, Neal,' she assured him.

They had pulled up at the house, and Neal turned off the engine and turned to her. 'Katie,' he croaked, 'if anything happened to Barbara I don't know what I'd do.' He banged the steering wheel with his fist. 'I should never have let her talk me into another baby,' he groaned.

'Neal,' she said. 'don't you want the baby?'

He glared at her. 'I want Barbara! Alive and well!' He put his head in his hands. 'God, Katie, wait'll you see her! She's so pale and weak.'

'Now you listen to me, Neal Evans,' Katherine said briskly. 'What's done is done. You won't help Barbara, or Nancy, or yourself, if you fall apart now. Above all else, Barbara needs to be free from worry. She's got enough on her mind. If you go around looking like a bedraggled rooster you'll only upset her.'

He was silent a minute, then looked at her sheepishly, a faint smile on his lips.

'You sound just like Mom,' he said weakly

'And you sound just like you did when you were ten,' she retorted. 'Come on, now, let's go.'

Meekly he obeyed her and followed her into the house. They were met at the door by an ecstatic Nancy, all dressed and ready to go in a short red princess coat and black patent leather mary janes.

'Oh, Aunt Katie, I'm going to South America!' she breathed. 'On an airplane, with Daddy!' Her eyes were wide with excitement.

Katherine stooped down and gave her a hug. 'And I see you're all ready to go, two hours ahead of time, just like your father.'

She turned and grinned at Neal, dressed in a dark business suit, tie a little askew. He managed a weak grin.

'Now,' she said, rising to her feet, 'fill me in on what needs to be done, and then I'll go say hello to Barbara.'

Neal began to explain to her what the doctor advised, and she listened carefully. Barbara was to get up *only* for the bathroom, nothing else.

'You'll have to be firm about that, Katie,' Neal

said emphatically, his face grim. 'She keeps wanting to get up.'

He showed her the sedative the doctor had ordered, only to be given if she became restless and unable to sleep. Any pains were to be reported to the doctor immediately. Neal had lettered a clear sign in his neat engineer's script with the doctor's and hospital's names and telephone numbers.

Then he filled her in on domestic details, the leaky tap in the laundry room he had been meaning to fix, the refrigerator and cupboard stocked with the food, dead bolt on both outside doors.

'I'm taking my car to the airport,' he said. 'Barbara's station wagon is in the garage. I've filled the tank and checked the tyres . . .'

'Neal,' Katherine broke in gently, 'it's almost time for you to leave. Are you packed?'

He looked at her in horror. 'Lord! No!' He bounded up the steps two at a time. Katherine followed him slowly. She couldn't help smiling to herself. She'd never seen him quite so beside himself.

She glanced back as she reached the bedroom landing. Little Nancy, in her red coat, was sitting patiently on a chair by the front door. She knows her father, Katherine thought. In his present state he's apt to leave without her if she doesn't plant herself where he can't miss her.

While Neal was in the bathroom throwing toilet articles in his bag, Katherine tiptoed into Barbara's room. The blinds were drawn and the small, still form of her sister-in-law was outlined on one side of the double bed, the black cropped head on the pillow. She seemed to be asleep.

Katherine noticed the dark smudges under her eyes, the pallor of her complexion, and her heart lurched with sudden anxiety. She was taking on a tremendous responsibility and she only hoped she wouldn't let them down.

'Katie,' Neal hissed at her from the hall. She went out to him. 'I've got to go now.' He gave his sleeping wife one last look filled with longing, then pecked Katherine on the cheek. 'Take good care of her, Sis.'

Katherine nodded solemnly. He squeezed her arm and ran downstairs. 'Don't forget Nancy,' she called after him softly from the top of the stairs. He hadn't. He waved at her, and they were gone.

Before going downstairs, she peeped into Barbara's room again. The still form was stirring.

'Katie,' Barbara called weakly, 'has he gone?'

Katherine stood by the side of the bed. 'Yes, Barbara, he's gone.'

'Thank goodness,' Barbara sighed, stretching a little and smiling. 'He was about to drive me crazy!' She took Katherine's hand and looked up at her. 'You'll never know how much I appreciate your coming like this. When I heard Neal tell his boss he couldn't go on this trip, I was frantic. I insisted he go.' She sighed and propped her head up higher on the pillows. 'I'm really fine. As long as I stay in bed there shouldn't be any problem. I'm pretty tough, really. But your brother seems to think I'm made of glass.' She grinned wickedly. 'Men!'

'Amen to that,' Katherine agreed, laughing. 'Now, can I get you anything?'

'I'd love a cup of coffee.'

'Coming right up!'

Katherine felt right at home in the comfortable kitchen where she had spent so much time in her childhood. Although Neal and Barbara had modernised the appliances and cabinet work, the room remained basically the same, even to her mother's dishtowels and tablecloths. And the cuckoo clock on the wall over the refrigerator.

As she moved about the familiar room making the coffee, getting out the spoons and mugs, she remembered how Neal and Luke had broken the cuckoo clock, still ticking away, but without the shrill-voiced little bird popping out to announce the hour.

They must have been about twelve, she thought, reminiscing, and she was eight. The clock, which had belonged to her grandmother, was keeping erratic time, the cuckoo appearing indiscriminately to announce the wrong hour. The two boys, both of them great tinkerers, had taken the clock apart one rainy afternoon when they had been alone in the house.

Katherine had come home from school to find them at the kitchen table staring down in perplexity at what seemed like a thousand tiny parts. She could see even now the two heads, one very blond, the other black, as they leaned over the table. She had gasped when she saw what they were doing, and Neal had given her one guilty look.

'If you tell, I'll break your arm,' he had threatened.

'She won't tell,' Luke had said confidently. 'She never does.'

Somehow, while she had sat and watched, entranced, they had put the clock back together, thanks mainly to Neal, the future engineer, but the cuckoo was gone for ever.

Now, as she carried the tray upstairs, Katherine smiled to herself at the memory. Barbara was lying propped up on her pillow, looking a little perkier now that her hovering husband was gone.

'What are you grinning at?' she asked as she took her mug from the tray. 'You look like the cat that swallowed the canary.'

'Not the canary,' Katherine replied, sitting down on the slipper chair beside the bed. 'The cuckoo.'

She told Barbara the story, hoping to amuse her and distract her mind from worry about the baby. Barbara chuckled appreciatively.

'Would Neal really have broken your arm?' she asked.

'No,' Katherine replied, laughing, 'but he might have given it a good twist.'

'Was he a bully?' Barbara asked. 'Did he make your life miserable? So many older brothers do.'

Katherine thought a minute. 'He liked to tease me, but on the whole he was pretty good to me. Occasionally, he and Luke would go off and leave me, but Luke would always come back and rescue me eventually. You see, he and I always had this kind of unspoken understanding between us, a kind of kinship that . . .'

She stopped short, colouring deeply, as she realised what she was saying, what she had been about to say. Recovering herself, she waved a hand and tried to pass it off. 'But you don't even know Luke, so I won't bore you with that.'

Barbara raised her eyebrows. 'Oh, yes, I know Luke. He's been to the house several times. Neal tells me he's going to buy his old home down the beach.'

Katherine only stared. 'I see,' she said at last in a small voice. 'I didn't know that.'

There was a silence between the two women as they drank their coffee. Katherine was shocked that Neal had resumed his friendship with Luke, even resentful. But then she realised she was being silly. Just because Luke hated her there was no reason why he and Neal shouldn't be friends.

'Katie,' Barbara said at last, 'what really happened between you and Brian Croft?'

Katherine got up and started pacing the room. 'Barbara, it's so long ago. I just want to forget it.'

'Sure, I understand. It's just that Neal and I weren't married until after you and Brian were divorced, and Neal has never told me what happened.'

Katherine stood at the foot of the bed, her hands gripping the railing. 'There's no reason why you shouldn't know. Brian only married me as a screen, a respectable façade for his real interest—other men.'

'Oh, Katie, how terrible for you! And you had no inkling before you married him?'

Katherine sighed. 'I don't think even he did, Barbara. He said he loved me. He was good-looking, kind, considerate. And after Luke rejected me I needed some gentle treatment.'

'After *Luke* rejected *you!*' Barbara exclaimed, her eyes wide. 'I thought it was the other way around.'

Katherine laughed harshly. 'Oh, that's Luke's version of it. He came home from college unexpectedly, after not calling or writing for months, and found me very tamely letting Brian kiss me goodnight after a dance. That was it.' She spread her hands in a gesture of helplessness. 'No halfway measures for Luke Dillon. It's all or nothing with him.'

'Yes,' Barbara said softly, 'I can see he's that kind of man.' Then she added, 'And that's why you still love him, isn't it?'

Before Katherine could reply, she saw that Barbara's eyes had closed. She must be worn out, Katherine thought. Softly, she picked up the tray and tiptoed out of the bedroom door.

As she rinsed out the dishes, she thought over her conversation with Barbara. She knew Barbara meant well, but it had opened wounds Katherine hoped were healing. Now she realised they were only festering underneath.

She walked out onto the deck. It was growing dark, the heavy bank of dark clouds obscuring the late afternoon sun. The water of the Sound was grey and heavy-looking, the sodden air oppressive and gloomy. Katherine leaned against the railing and stared out at the dripping fir trees, the wet greyish-coloured beach, and wondered in despair what she was going to do.

Gradually she felt a little calmer. A wind came up, ruffling the water and sighing through the trees. It was so peaceful here, she thought. It had been good for her, she realised suddenly, to talk to Barbara about Brian, her marriage, about Luke.

Barbara was right: she did love Luke. Even when she hated him and fought against him, she had loved him. He was like a part of herself. But even as she admitted this to herself, she knew she could never have him. Oh, he desired her physically, as she desired him. But in his desire was the need to hurt, to wound, to get revenge. That wasn't love.

The next few days were sunny, with a cold, crisp fall brightness that cast lacy shadows through the giant evergreens. Katherine was busy, running errands, cleaning, fixing meals, visiting with Barbara whenever she felt strong enough for company.

Barbara's colour had improved, and her spirits seemed better each day. Soon Katherine began to worry that she'd have a hard time keeping her in bed. But she needn't have. Barbara was determined to keep this baby.

'To the bathroom and back, and that's it,' she said firmly.

Neal called from Buenos Aires early on Saturday evening. She reassured him that everything was fine, that there were no problems, and Barbara seemed to be getting stronger every day.

Barbara got on the bedroom extension, and Katherine smiled to herself as she heard Neal's voice before she hung up. 'Darling, I miss you so much and love you more than I can say.' That didn't sound like her brusque, impatient, offhand brother.

When the long conversation was over, Barbara was exhausted. 'That man!' she exclaimed wearily when Katherine took her supper up to her. 'If he really loved me, he wouldn't fret so. He wears me out with his fussing. It takes all my strength to reassure *him*!'

'Neal really loves you, Barbara, believe me,' Katherine said with a smile. 'He just comes on a little too strong sometimes.'

Barbara's eyes began to close as soon as she finished eating. Katherine took the tray downstairs and straightened up the kitchen. It was seven o'clock and dark outside.

She glanced through the evening paper as she finished her coffee and decided to watch a movie on television at eight. She went upstairs, showered, and put on her heavy red velour robe, zipping it up at the front to her neck.

On the way downstairs, she peeped in at Barbara. She was sound asleep, breathing peacefully. In the living room, she decided to make a fire. Then she switched on the dim television lamp, turned on the set and settled down for the evening.

The doorbell rang, and, startled, she jumped up and ran to the door. 'Who is it?' she called. She tried to fight down her anxiety. It was a deserted spot, two women alone, one of them helpless.

'It's me,' came a deep voice. 'Luke.'

Katherine's heart turned over. With trembling

fingers she unlatched the door and pulled it open. He stood on the porch, his expression sober and inscrutable. Then the dark eyes looked her up and down, and she realised she was in her robe and nothing else. It was a heavy robe, she thought defensively. He couldn't misconstrue that as an invitation.

'What are you doing here?' she asked blankly.

'Do you mind if I come in? It's cold out here.' His voice was heavy with sarcasm. She let him in and shut the door. He took off his heavy leather jacket and threw it on a chair. 'Neal called me before he left and asked me to look in on Barbara. How is she?'

So that was it, she thought. He had only come out of duty to Neal. She felt a little twinge of disappointment. She followed him into the living room. He was standing with his back to the fire, long legs wide apart, hands clasped behind his back. He had on dark trousers, a pale blue shirt and a loose-fitting dark pullover.

He's so tall, she thought, as she walked over to the television set and switched it off. She could sense his eyes following her every move, watchful, appraising. His very presence in the room set her pulses racing, her blood tingling.

'She's fine,' she said at last. 'A little weak, but resting comfortably.' She hesitated, then looked up at him. 'It was kind of you to come.'

Luke raised an eyebrow sardonically and grinned. 'I must admit I had other motives.' His insinuating dark eyes swept over her.

Katherine purposely misunderstood him. 'Yes,'

she said. 'I hear you've decided to buy back your old house. Does that mean you intend to stay in Seattle, to join the firm?' If so, she vowed to herself sadly, I'll have to leave.

'I haven't decided yet,' he said. 'I may stay in New York and use this as a summer place.' His eyes bored into her. Even clear across the room from him his eyes had the power to compel her. 'What would you like me to do?'

She forced out a little laugh. 'I? I don't see what I have to do with it.'

'Don't you?' His grin was complacent. 'Have you forgotten? You and I have some unfinished business to settle.'

She stared at him. 'You're crazy,' she said. 'Do you mean to say that you're going to stake your whole future career on—on—getting me into bed?'

He shrugged. 'Why not? I've proved what I can do in the law. I have plenty of money. Everybody needs a hobby.' He grinned wickedly.

Katherine was speechless. To carry revenge that far was insane! He hadn't changed. Beneath the smooth, polished, sophisticated exterior was the same wild boy who was a law unto himself.

'Come here, Katie,' he said, his voice low, inviting. 'Put us both out of our misery.'

'I don't know what you mean,' she said weakly, turning away from him.

'Damn it,' he growled, 'quit playing games with me!'

In four long strides he was across the room standing before her, his powerful hands gripping her shoulders. His eyes were wild as he glared down into hers, his broad chest heaving. Electric sparks seemed to dance between them in the few inches of space that separated them.

Her eyes pleaded with him. 'Please, Luke, leave me alone,' she begged. 'Just leave me in peace.'

For answer, his mouth came down hard on hers. For a moment she resisted, tried to pull away, but his vice-like grip on her shoulders held her fast. As he pulled her close, she could feel the full length of his hard muscular body pressing against her own.

With a little groan she allowed herself to respond to his kiss. Her lips softened and parted under his and she reached around his waist to hold him, her hands slipping under his sweater to the thin cotton shirt underneath.

Luke shivered at her touch, then tore his mouth from hers and looked deeply into her eyes, one hand cupping her chin, his long fingers pressed along the line of her jaw.

'Do you still want me to leave, Katie?' he whispered.

She shook her head, lost now in the wonder of his embrace, uncaring about the future. 'No. Don't go,' she said.

He sighed deeply, then, still holding her chin, he kissed her softly, gently, his mouth barely brushing hers, teasing her lips until she longed for a deeper kiss. She pulled his shirt-tail out of his trousers and ran her hands up the smooth firm skin of his back, feeling the muscles ripple under her touch.

Now his kiss became firmer, demanding, penetrating, insistent. With his mouth still on hers he picked her up and carried her upstairs.

CHAPTER NINE

HE knew her old bedroom, of course, which was at the other end of the hall from Barbara's. He laid her gently down on the bed. He left the door into the hall slightly open so that the light glowed dimly into the bedroom, then he sat down beside her, leaning over her. His eyes were half closed, but the expression on his face, in the set of his mouth, was triumphant.

Katherine didn't care. She was tired of fighting him. She knew he didn't love her, could never love her as he once had with that same implicit trust and single-minded devotion. Still, she didn't care. She had always wanted him, and it seemed somehow fitting that the consummation of their passion was to take place here, the scene of their childhood. They had come full circle back to the past.

Slowly, Luke reached out and smoothed her long golden hair away from her face so that it was spread out on the pillow. Then he moved his hands down her body, over her heavy robe, passing lightly over her shoulders, lingering for a moment at her breast, then down to her thighs.

In one quick motion he pulled the dark sweater over his head and tossed it on the bed. Slowly he unbuttoned his shirt, revealing the bare muscular chest with its light covering of dark hair. Then he reached out and pulled the zipper of her robe down from her neck to her hips. He parted the opening to bare her breast, then gently lowered the upper half of his body down on hers and kissed her.

The feel of his bare skin on hers made Katherine shiver with ecstasy, and as his mouth covered hers she groaned deep in her throat. He moved over on his side after a moment and began to fondle her breasts, teasing the nipples until they hardened.

Their eyes met in the dimness. Katherine longed to declare her love. The dear familiar face with its hard features softened now in passion was so full of desire, his hands on her body so gentle even in their demanding exploration, that she had to remind herself that he was only using her. But she didn't care. She wanted him, and if this was the only way she could ever possess him, it was worth it.

Then his hand still kneading the round soft fullness, he took one pink tip into his mouth, sending flames shooting through her so that she reached out blindly, cradling the dark head, pressing it tighter to her breast, her hands clutching wildly at the crisp dark hair at the back of his neck.

Luke made an almost animalistic sound and in a frenzy pulled his mouth and hands away, tore off his shirt, then pulled the robe from her shoulders. Katherine sat up so he could free her arms, and then he was holding her, their lips glued together, their hands frantically searching, exploring each other's bodies.

Just as he reached one hand down to unbuckle the belt of his trousers, a faint voice from down the hall called out, 'Katherine!' It was Barbara. They broke apart, staring at each other.

'Hell!' Luke growled. 'What was that?'

They sat there on the bed listening. Then it came again. 'Katie!'

'It's Barbara,' said Katherine. 'I've got to go to her.' She twisted into her robe and zipped it up, then got off the bed, heading for the door.

He came up behind her and put his hands on her waist. 'You'll come back?' he whispered in her ear. His hands slid up and roughly possessed her breasts.

She sighed with pleasure and murmured her willing assent, leaning back against him for a second to signify her surrender. Then she broke away and ran down the hall to Barbara's room.

She was propped up on one elbow. In the light from the beside lamp, Katherine could see the ghastly pallor of her face, the features twisted in pain. She ran to the bed and knelt down beside it.

'What is it, Barbara?' she murmured. She felt her forehead. It was clammy with perspiration.

'I think you'd better call Dr Pierce,' Barbara groaned. 'I'm in trouble!'

Katherine ran down to the kitchen telephone where she had put Neal's instructions. Luke was in the kitchen fully dressed. He had warmed the coffee and was pouring himself a cup. When she burst in he took in her anxious eyes and trembling hands in one sweeping glance and reached out to her.

'What is it, darling?'

She looked up at him grateful for the strength of his strong hand on her arm. 'She's in trouble. I've got to call the doctor.'

He nodded and released her arm. She found Dr

Pierce's number and dialled. A woman's voice answered, curt and businesslike.

'This is Dr Pierce's answering service. May I help you?'

'I must speak to Dr Pierce right away. I'm calling for Mrs Neal Evans. Barbara Evans.'

'One moment, please.' There was a short silence. Then, 'I'm sorry, Dr Pierce is in Spokane at the State Medical Convention. He left instructions for Mrs Evans to go directly to the hospital emergency room at any indication of trouble. Do you have that number?'

Katherine repeated the number Neal had given her. 'That is correct,' said the voice.

'Thank you,' Katherine mumbled, and hung up.

She dialled the hospital's number and told them she was bringing Barbara in. They said they would be ready for her and gave her instructions where to go.

She ran up the stairs, her robe flapping around her ankles, apprehensive about having left Barbara alone for so long. She burst into the bedroom to find Luke sitting on the edge of the bed, gently wiping Barbara's face with a washcloth, his other hand holding hers.

'Feel better now, Barbara?' he asked. His voice was low and steady, with a gentleness in it Katherine had never heard before.

Katherine stood in the doorway and stared, watching this tender Luke she never knew existed. Barbara's breath came in short gasps, but there was a weak smile on her face.

'Luke,' Katherine called. He turned to her. 'I've got to take her to the hospital.'

He thought for a second. 'Do they know she's coming?' She nodded. 'All right. Help me get a coat on her. Then you go and get dressed. I'll carry her down to the car. We'll use her station wagon so she can lie down. Bring some blankets and a pillow.'

Katherine found a warm coat in Barbara's closet. She and Luke carefully got Barbara into it, Luke supporting her with a strong arm and Katherine guiding her arms into the sleeves. Then she raced down the hall and quickly tore off her robe. She threw on a pair of blue denims and a checked shirt and grabbed her heavy wool jacket. She found blankets and an extra pillow in the hall closet.

When she got downstairs, Luke was waiting at the front door holding Barbara in his powerful arms as though she was a feather. Barbara's head rested on his shoulder, her eyes closed.

They managed to lay her down in the back of the station wagon without jostling her around too much, then Katherine handed Luke the car keys and got in the back with Barbara. Luke got into the driver's seat, checked out the controls briefly, then started the engine and drove up to the main road. In a few minutes he turned on the heat, and soon the back of the car was warm.

Luke drove fast, but smoothly, and Katherine hardly noticed the bumps and curves. She held Barabara's hand and prayed, suddenly overwhelmed with her awesome responsibility. If anything happened to Barbara, Neal would never forgive her.

She glanced ahead at Luke's dark head and broad shoulders and realised suddenly in a rush of gratitude that she would never have been able to do this without him. The hospital would have had to send an ambulance, and in Barbara's condition, any delay could mean disaster.

At the hospital Luke pulled the station wagon up in front of the emergency entrance and got out of the car. As Katherine opened the back door, she heard a man's voice call out.

'Hey, mister, you can't park there. You're blocking the entrance!'

'The hell I can't!' Luke barked, and was beside Katherine in a few long strides. He lifted his head and called back to the man. 'Go and get someone with a stretcher and then I'll move the car.'

Katherine stood aside as Luke bent over and gently lifted Barbara out of the back seat. In the light coming from the hospital her face looked greenish. Her eyes were closed, her mouth half open, her breath coming in short rasping gasps. Katherine was glad that Neal wasn't here to see her like this.

Two men with a trolley appeared at the side of the car. Luke carried Barbara over to it and placed her carefully on the narrow bed. The two men strapped her in and started wheeling the trolley up the ramp, while Katherine ran ahead to give them the necessary information about Barbara and get her admitted. She watched them wheel her into the emergency room and answered the attendant's questions with a faltering voice.

After Luke had moved the car he came into the wide corridor where Katherine was sitting wearily on the long bench that ran almost the whole length of the hall. He crossed over to her quickly, sat down beside her and without a word, took her hand in his.

They sat there in silence for almost half an hour. In spite of her concern for Barbara, Katherine felt that she had never loved Luke so much as she did now. In the most unromatic of settings, with the harsh glare of the hospital lighting draining them of colour, the strength that came to her from the large hand holding hers filled her with gratitude and love.

At last, a young interne, dressed in a rumpled white uniform, came out of the emergency room and looked around. Katherine rose quickly to her feet and rushed over to him.

'I'm Mrs Evans' sister-in-law. How is she?'

The young doctor looked exhausted, but he managed a faint grin. 'She'll be okay. We'll keep her here for a day or two until Dr Pierce gets back.

'How about the baby?' Katherine asked.

He frowned. 'It's touch and go,' he said. Then he grinned again. 'But never underestimate the power of the will to live, even in the unborn. They're tenacious little critters from the moment of conception!'

'Thank you, doctor,' said Katherine as he turned and walked slowly away. There was hope! She felt such an intense relief that she began to slump. Strong arms reached around her shoulders, holding her up, pulling her against a broad chest. She looked up to see Luke smiling down at her.

'Oh, Luke, she's going to be all right!' she breathed. 'I'm so relieved!'

'I know, I know,' he murmured, holding her close. He kissed her forehead lightly and smoothed back her hair from her forehead. 'Come on, let's go.'

He drove back slowly to Neal's house. Katherine's head was on his shoulder, her hand on his knee. When they arrived she was almost asleep. He switched off the car engine and looked down at her, and sleepily she raised her eyes to his.

'Go on inside, now,' he said, 'and get some sleep. I'll come over tomorrow.'

She nodded and slipped out of the car. She went to the door of the house and was thankful she had remembered to lock it. The porch light was on. Luke had got into his own car and started it, but he leaned out now and called to her.

'Everything okay?' he asked.

Katherine waved at him and he drove off. She locked and bolted the door behind her and went up to her room. As she got undressed she noticed that Luke's dark sweater was still on her bed where he had thrown it earlier.

She picked it up and held it against her cheek. With her eyes closed she could almost imagine the rough texture of the wool was Luke's cheek against hers, and as she breathed in the masculine smell of it, her heart ached with love. Then, feeling foolish, she folded the sweater neatly and set it on the dresser. She got into bed, switched off the light, and was asleep instantly.

In the light of day, as Katherine sat at the kitchen counter eating breakfast, the events of the night before seemed unreal, dreamlike, as if they had happened to someone else or she had read about it in a book.

Yet Barbara was gone and Luke's sweater was still on her dressing table where she had placed it last night. As she sipped her coffee meditatively and looked out at the pale October sunlight dancing on the dark blue Sound, Katherine's thoughts were all of Luke and what in the world she was going to do about the situation she had got herself into. After all my fine resolutions, she thought wryly, there I was ready to climb into bed with him at the crook of his little finger!

She sighed and poured herself another cup of coffee. She had called the hospital first thing. Barbara was resting comfortably and all was well so far. She wondered how Neal would react to the news. Probably hop the first plane back and to hell with the job.

How she envied them! They were so right for each other, understood each other so well, had built such a solid relationship based on love and trust and respect. She and Luke had been right for each other once, she thought sadly. But then the trust had gone. It wasn't in him to ever trust her again, and without trust there could be no love, only a physical desire.

Still, she thought, as she went to the sink and rinsed out her cup, wasn't such a powerful sexual attraction a sort of basis for a relationship? Sure, she thought bitterly, a short one. Did she really want that? She dried her hands and went out on to the deck.

She leaned on the railing drinking in the balmy salt-tanged air. An Indian summer day, she thought. She had on the same blue denims she had worn last night and a thin cotton shirt. The sight of the calm water and smooth deserted beach gave her a feeling of peace in spite of her confusion about Luke.

Then, to the right, out of the corner of her eye, she caught sight of a tall figure striding down the beach. She stared. It was Luke. Her heart started to pound. He must have stayed in his old house last night, she thought. He had said he was going to buy it.

He was looking up at her. He waved briefly. Katherine waved back and waited for him. Soon he was coming up the path from the beach in long graceful strides, the powerful muscles of his thighs straining against his dark trousers. He had on a white knit shirt, open at the neck, and as he came closer Katherine could see that he was freshly shaven.'

'How's the patient this morning?' he asked as he stepped on to the deck.

'She's doing fine—thanks to you.'

Luke raised an eyebrow. 'I'm not the doctor. Thank him.'

He was so close to her now that she could smell his faint aftershave, see the little spot near his left ear that the razor had missed. He didn't touch her, but he seemed to sense her confusion.

'How about a cup of coffee?' he said lightly.

'Of course. Come inside.'

He leaned back against the refrigerator watching her as she made a fresh pot of coffee. She could feel his eyes boring into her as she fumbled nervously at the sink.

'You must have stayed in your old house last night,' she remarked casually. 'I didn't know you'd already bought it.'

'I haven't. I'm renting it by the week from the owner's estate.'

'Then you haven't made up your mind yet what you're going to do.'

'Yes, I have.' He paused. 'I've decided to leave New York and join the firm here.'

Katherine's heart turned over. 'I see,' she said evenly as she measured out the coffee with trembling fingers.

'You don't sound overjoyed,' Luke remarked dryly.

She took a deep breath and turned to face him. 'It's none of my business what you do. It's just that if you join the firm I'll have to leave.'

He frowned. 'Why in hell would you do that?'

She shrugged and turned away. 'It's obvious, isn't it? We can't even get along on a temporary basis.' To herself, she added, and I couldn't bear to see you every day, loving you, knowing how you despised me, seeing you with Selma.

In one long stride he was beside her. He grabbed her by the shoulders and wheeled her aound to face him. 'Now, what's that supposed to mean?' he barked. 'It seems to me we were getting along just fine last night.'

Katherine opened her mouth to reply when his head bent swiftly and his lips were on hers. His mouth tasted of toothpaste, fresh and clean, demanding and rough. She pushed at his chest. He released her lips, stood back and glared down at her, his hands still gripping her shoulders.

'Stop it, Luke,' she begged. 'Let's stop playing games.'

Her voice was weary, her defences shattered. 'If you want me to sleep with you, I will. Then your revenge will be complete. That's what you want, isn't it?'

His dark eyes were wide with amazement. 'You're crazy!' he exclaimed, shaking her a little. 'What do I have to do to convince you that I love you, that I've always loved you, only you?'

She turned her head away. 'Oh, Luke, don't! You don't treat a woman the way you've treated me if you love her. Be honest with me.'

'Sit down,' he commanded imperiously. She looked at him warily. 'Go on,' he growled, 'sit down.' He pulled her over to the kitchen table, pushed her down on a chair, then sat next to her.

'Now listen to me,' he said, leaning towards her. 'When I found you kissing Brian Croft that night I came home from college, my whole world came crashing down around my head. You *were* my whole world. I *trusted* you!'

Katherine buried her face in her hands, unable to endure the sight of that beloved face, so tormented, so close to her own. 'I know, I know,' she wailed. Then she looked at him. 'But you never wrote, you never called. I know you were swamped with all you had to do, but, Luke, I was so young, and so stupid.'

'Well, at least you admit that,' he said gruffly.

'Oh, I'll admit anything,' she cried wildly. 'Just put me in a witness chair and I'll plead guilty to any accusation you want to make. But, Luke, I've paid and paid and paid. Believe me, you don't know!'

He put a hand on her cheek. 'Yes, I do know, now.'

Katherine hesitated a moment. She hated to break the spell, but she had to know. She looked into his eyes. 'Why, Luke?' she asked gently. 'Why did you just walk out of my life like that?' She sighed. 'All those years wasted!'

He turned his head away so that she could just see the mouth set in a grim line, the pulse throbbing below his ear. He ran a hand through his dark hair and groaned softly.

'Pride, I guess, just about sums it up.' With an effort he turned to face her. Her heart went out to him when she saw the pain in his eyes.

'At first,' he went on slowly, carefully, measuring each word, 'before I saw you with Brian that night, I barely had five minutes a day to call my own. There was the studying, the job, the football. And,' his voice faltered, 'I just took it for granted that you were as deeply committed to me as I was to you. It was agony not being able to see you or hold you. We'd been like one person all our lives. Letters and phone calls would only have made it worse.'

'But I *was* committed . . .' she began.

'I know that now!' he almost shouted. 'Remember, I was just a kid, too.' His eyes softened. 'You didn't have a monopoly on stupidity. I should have written or called once in a while.'

Katherine took his hand in hers and raised it to her lips. 'But what about afterwards?' she murmured against it. 'Why didn't you answer my letters, talk to me, let me explain?'

Luke stood up and began pacing around the room, his hands shoved in his pockets. 'At first,' he began, 'just the thought of Brian Croft with his hands on you drove me wild. For a long time I just brooded, half out of my mind with jealousy—and, as I said, pride. If you recall, I could be stubborn on occasion. I guess I wanted to hurt you the way you hurt me.' His back was to her now and he stood staring out the window. 'Then, later, there was a girl.' He turned around. 'In fact, as time went on, several girls.'

Her first reaction to his words was a sudden rush of blind unreasoning jealousy. Her mouth flew open and her hands clenched into fists, her fingernails digging painfully into the palms of her hands. She was stunned.

At the sight of her stricken face, Luke crossed the room swiftly and knelt down at her side. He cupped his hands around her face and forced her to look at him.

'Katie, listen to me. I swear that not one woman I've ever known found her way into my heart but you. Hell,' he added, 'what did you expect? I was a big football hero, a fine trophy for the little sorority girls, then a rising young lawyer. I denied myself the one thing I really wanted—you—shoved all thought of you down inside so deep I thought I'd never have to look at it again. So I decided not to deny myself anything else that struck my fancy or came my way. Then, by the time I realised every other girl was only a pale substitute for what I really wanted, you were married to Brian.'

He jumped abruptly to his feet and looked down at her with wild eyes. 'God, when I think how I've treated you, how I've wanted you, never stopped wanting . . . Katie, can you forgive me?'

She stood up and put her hands on his shoulders. 'Forgive you, Luke?' she asked. 'I love you. Love forgives everything.'

He put his arms around her and crushed her to him. Then he pulled away and looked down deeply into her eyes. 'We'll get married right away.'

'Yes, darling,' she said meekly. Then she grinned mischievously. 'That is, if you're sure Selma won't mind.'

'Selma!' Luke exclaimed. 'She means nothing to me.'

'It didn't look that way to me,' she remarked.

'Listen, I haven't lived an exactly celibate life these past ten years, but I always drew the line at married women—even those with so-called "open" marriage. Which, by the way, is definitely *out* for us.'

'Yes, darling,' Katherine murmured again, re-assured.

Slowly his mouth lowered to hers, and once again she tasted its sweetness. His kiss was gentle and loving, but soon, as their sensual awareness of each other became more acute, his mouth opened and

took fuller possession of hers,exploring it insistently.

Panting, she leaned her head back. Luke's
mouth moved to her neck, her throat, up under her
ears. Her hair had fallen down and he clutched at it
with one hand, pulling her head back even further,
bracing her against the hand. His other hand was at
her breast now, caressing and fumbling with the
buttons of her shirt.

Then, gently, he moved the open shirt aside. She
had on a wispy lacy low-cut bra, virtually trans-
parent. She heard his gasp as his eyes drank her in,
then felt his hand on the half-exposed breast,
kneading it gently, slipping his thumb inside the
flimsy material to move gently, teasingly over the
hardening nipple.

Then he scooped her up and carried her up to her
bedroom. He set her down and slipped the shirt off
her shoulders. As it fell to the ground Katherine
stood proudly before him, head held high, shoulders back, waiting for him, loving the look in his
eyes as he gazed at her.

He pulled off his shirt, then gently turned her
around so that he stood behind her. Deftly he
unhooked the bra. She leaned slightly forward to
shrug off the straps from her shoulders and felt his
hands move to cup the full breasts. She sighed and
leaned back against his bare chest, loving the feel of
his hands on her, tingling as they stroked and
caressed more insistently.

Luke found the zipper of her denim pants, and
she shuddered with desire as his hands moved down
over her abdomen and hips to pull them off, linger-

ing on the sensitive skin of her inner thighs.

Then she heard his own trousers come off. He pressed himself against her, and she felt for the first time his male hardness. He made a noise deep in his throat and turned her around, and they stood naked before each other. He looked into her eyes, as if searching her very soul.

'Do you want to wait, Katie?' he choked. 'Until after we're married?'

'No,' she whispered. 'We've already waited too long.'

He guided her to the bed and gently eased her down on her back. He stood for a moment looking down at her, his eyes sweeping her body from head to toe. Then he eased himself down on top of her, and as he took full possession of her at last, the rockets exploded in her head, and she cried out just as her whole body gave a tremendous final shudder of release, she knew that she hadn't waited for him in vain. They had come full circle, she thought, as she cradled his dark head against her breast, and now the circle was closed for ever.